Seduced by Dragons

Lilly Wilder

Published by Lilly Wilder, 2023.

Table of Contents

Seduced by Dragons

By: Lilly Wilder

Foreword

I thought he was just an asshole – a sexy asshole – but an asshole all the same.

Turns out he's a dragon.

And there are hundreds of them living in the woods, hidden away from human society.

They're split into two clans: the Aetos and the Ragnis.

And I'm the key to total warfare between them.

Why?

Because someone wants me, and he can't have me.

Did I happen to mention that this is the same asshole I vowed to hate for the rest of my life?

Yeah, it's complicated.

To make matters worse, there was another guy thrown into the mix.

Vern is cute and funny – everything a girl could ever want.

But to have him, I have to have them both.

They both need me to breed for their clan.

Buy Lyle Stokes will always be my enemy.

The only thing that might be stronger than my hate for Lyle is my craving for Vern.

Seduced by Dragons

Chapter 1 Ari

Thump. Thump. Thump.

Music thrummed through my ears. My heartbeat kept with the tempo. Beads of sweat gathered along my brow. I swept them away with a swipe of my arm as I continued through the park.

Along the way, I passed a couple of old-time joggers. They had upped their game by including 2-pound weights to their power walks. Chirpy as always, they waved in greeting. I returned the wave with one of my own.

Distracted as I was, I didn't have enough time to react to the person who had suddenly popped up in front of me. I tried to veer to the left, but I wasn't quick enough. I barreled straight into his chest.

The force of it was enough to send me crashing into the ground. Luckily, I landed on my ass. Thanks to my fair share of squats, it was a decent-enough cushion.

A second later, I felt the air being knocked out of my lungs.

"Oof!" I gasped as I was pinned to the ground by someone's weight.

As we tried to get up, all we managed was a tangling of limbs.

"Oh dear, should we do something Geraldine?" One of the old women looked on with a look of concern painted on her face.

"Oh no," answered Geraldine, "it looks like they're having their fair share of fun." She jabbed her friend with her elbow. "Do you remember when we were young?" A giggle erupted from her lips. "Oh! The trouble we caused!"

Laughing, the two women walked away to continue their afternoon exercise.

Meanwhile, I was still trying to free myself from this rather embarrassing situation. "I'm starting to think you like it on top of me," I huffed. As I spoke, I got my first real look at the stranger.

Whoa.

He had this charming smile – you know, the kind of smile you might find on the cover of a magazine. "I must admit, it's a rather nice view," he said with a wink.

I expected him to be staring at my chest or something but he was looking straight into my eyes. He had such intensity to his gaze that it made me feel like I was the only girl in the entire world. It made me shiver.

"Mommy? What are they doing?" A little kid pointed in our direction.

"Looks like that kid is going to be hearing about the birds and the bees," the stranger chuckled.

"Are you ever going to get off me?"

"I'm thinking about it but it's a shame when you're so damn comfy."

Was this guy serious right now? We were in a public park for crying out loud. But, at the same time, I could have been making a bigger fuss about the whole thing and I wasn't. Truth be told, I was rather enjoying myself. It's not every day that a drop-dead gorgeous man falls right into your lap.

"Alright, foot patrol's giving us a funny look. We better get up before we get charged for public indecency." Finally, he rose to his feet and offered a hand.

I took it and with the utmost ease, he lifted me off the ground. Since he was wearing nothing but a tank top, I could see his ripped muscles underneath the skin of his arm.

Wow.

This guy definitely worked out. There was no doubt about it.

And it didn't stop at his arm. The thin fabric of his shirt did little to hide the lean of his torso.

"Hope I didn't hurt you," he said, voice husky, as soon as the foot cop passed us by. "You just kind of barreled right into me. I've heard of love at first sight, but I'd say you're taking it a bit too literally, don't you think?"

I blushed at his words. "What?"

He grinned. "I'm just teasing. It's something I do." Without warning, he grabbed my hand and started running. I had no choice but to follow his lead or risk getting dragged along.

It only took a few seconds for us to fall into a perfect sync. "What do you think you're doing?" I said in protest but I continued to follow him along the path.

"I've always wanted to do that!" He shouted as he picked up the pace. We were running at a full-blown spirit. My calf muscles ached with exertion but still, I kept going. Our palms had become so sweaty that we were forced to let go of one another. Free to pump my arms, I urged myself to run a little faster, pulling ahead of the mysterious stranger.

Honestly, this whole thing was absolutely insane. What was I even doing? Then again, what was the harm in having a bit of fun every once in a while?

"Oh, it's a race, is it?" He growled. "You're on!" He charged ahead and I swear he didn't even break a sweat doing it.

I cursed under my breath and struggled to keep up. And I thought I was good at running. This guy had to be a professional or something.

He cruised to a large oak tree and stopped there like it had been designated as our finish line. By the time I caught up, there was this dirty grin on his face. "Not bad, not bad."

"Who the hell are you?" I panted for breath.

"Name's Vern," he introduced himself with one of his charming smiles.

My legs were already jelly but he was definitely making it worse.

"I'm... Ari." I doubled over and gasped for air. "Jeez... I guess I'm out of shape."

"Nah, I'm just incredibly good," he responded with a wink. "I'm amazed you were able to keep up as much as you did."

"I can see that having an ego is one of your charming characteristics," I huffed sarcastically. "You know, there's something called modesty in this world. It's pretty attractive."

"Is it now?" He raised an eyebrow. "I've never heard of it."

"I guess you learn something new every day," I returned.

"Guess so." Again, there was that charming smile of his. It had my heart jumping through hoops. An overwhelming heat lingered just behind my cheeks. Desperate to quench the fire, I jogged over to a nearby water fountain.

The cool, refreshing stream worked wonders.

"Take your time, take your time," Vern mused as he stood behind me.

It was then that I felt the weight of his stare. I whipped around and narrowed my eyes with suspicion. "Were you just staring at my ass?"

"Sorry. Guilty as charged," he answered with a grin. "But can you really blame me? That's quite the asset."

"Oh wow." I groaned. "Are you looking to win the lamest joke of the year?"

"Maybe." He stepped forward. "Or maybe I'm just giving you a compliment."

"You know, I really should slap you for being such a pig."

"Who's stopping you?" He challenged. He even turned his cheek to make it easier for me. This guy was something else entirely. If I didn't know any better, I'd say he was an alien. "But here's what I think," his voice was a low, seductive whisper, "I think you're completely smitten by me but you just don't want to admit it."

I was so entranced by the smoothness of his voice that I did not notice his fingertips dancing along the length of my arm. It was only when I looked down, did I see that he had me by the elbows.

His grin deepened as he pulled me closer. Our bodies were mere inches apart.

I held my breath.

"C'mon, you don't have to play hard to get with me."

Suddenly, I came crashing back to reality. I pushed away and shook my head. "Are you always this forward?"

"Only on Tuesdays."

"But today's Thursday," I answered. "Oh! What does it matter? You're clearly a crazy person."

"Am I?" He had me pinned up against a tree in a moment's notice. "Because I don't hear you screaming. If you really thought I was a crazy person, you'd try to get away from me."

"I did!" I protested as I jerked against his grip. His fingers tightened to a vice-like hold. "And how do you expect me to get away when you have me trapped?"

"All you have to do is ask and I'll let go." He leaned forward ever so slightly so that his warm breath brushed against the side of my neck. I shivered as a euphoric sensation traveled just underneath my skin. It seemed to fester inside my chest, forcing my heart to work in double time.

I looked up and our eyes locked.

What was this guy doing to me? It was like he had cast some sort of magical spell that was making me act weird.

"Admit it, you like it here." He was about to continue but I interrupted him with a knee to the groin.

He fell away, gasping. "Now, was that really necessary?"

"Maybe next time you'll think twice about acting like a creep," I said.

Thinking our time together was over, I went over to a bench and tied my shoe. A second later, there he was. This guy just couldn't take a hint, could he? Then again, I wasn't trying very hard to get him to leave me alone. Maybe he was right. Maybe I liked him for whatever crazy reason. And now I'm just being ridiculous. There's no way I like this guy. We only just met.

"For fear of having you knee me a second time, let's talk about something a bit less scandalous."

"Who says I want to talk to you at all?"

"The cat has claws." He placed a hand on his chest and feigned injury.

I laughed. "And you're overdramatic."

"Admit it, you like that about me."

"What's up with this obsession over whether I like you or not? You know, most guys take a girl out on a date and get to know her –"

"Alright, how about The Shoppe?" He pointed his thumb in its direction. "If you ask me, it has the best coffee in town."

"Not a chance."

"Ouch! Way to crush my dreams."

"I'm sorry but after our little race, I'm way too sweaty to be seen in public."

"I hate to tell you this but we're in public now." He held out his arms, motioning to the park.

"Yeah, well, this is different. No one is sitting close enough to smell me."

"So, I'm chopped liver now?"

"Pretty much." This whole interaction was so bizarre, it felt like a dream. This guy couldn't be real. No one actually acted this way. He was like some hunk out of a movie. So, why was I playing along with his little game? Perhaps I had finally lost my mind.

To keep my sanity, I continued on my run but like a bad curse, there he was again.

"I'm starting to think you're a stalker."

"If you did, you would have called on the police to help you." He pointed at the foot patrol officers as we ran past them.

He had a point. For whatever reason, it was almost like I trusted this man. I had no reason to but I guess it was his easy going and playful manner that had me reeled like a bass on a hook.

"Alright, well, I really need to get going. I can't have you following me home."

"Drats, and just when I thought I was making progress, too." He snapped his fingers together before reaching into his pocket. He pulled out a permanent market.

Before I could stop him, he took my arm and wrote his number on it. "I work at Thirsty Sage Lounge."

"The bar on the avenue?" I asked.

"That's the one. So, if you ever want a drink, you know where to find me." He snapped the cap back on.

I was about to ask him something but all of a sudden, he had vanished. I blinked, thinking maybe it was just a figment of my imagination but no, he was really gone. This day was just getting weirder and weirder...

Chapter 2 Ari

I came home and took a much-needed shower. It felt incredibly good to feel the water cascading down my body. I scrubbed away the sweat and grime that had accumulated during the day.

As my hands passed over my breasts, I gasped. A vivid fantasy of Vern popped into my head. He was standing there with me. Plastered on his face was that wild grin of his. And below that... well, let's just say my mind conjured up the body of a Greek god. His skin was taut with the muscle hiding underneath and his abdomen seemed to be chiseled from the finest stone.

My cheeks burned as my mind wandered further south to the package between his legs. I bit my bottom lip.

Suddenly, the water turned cold and my little daydream came to a halting end. Quickly, I got out of the shower and wrapped a towel around my body.

What was that?

Sure, Vern was handsome but was he really that handsome that I would start fantasizing about him in my shower? Something was seriously wrong with me.

I tried to push him away from my mind but he kept cropping back up again. It was like he had infected my head with that smile of his. I had honestly never felt an attraction this strong before.

As I tussled my hair dry, I realized I had scrubbed away his number from my arm. Well, there goes that idea. Now, if I wanted to see him again, I'd have to go to the bar and I really didn't like bars all that much. Most of the time, the counters were all sticky and the men even sticker.

"I just need to forget about him," I whispered to myself. "Today was a fluke. In all honesty, I'll probably never see him again." But those words dismayed me. My heart ached like a boa constrictor had wound itself around the organ. It was almost like he had taken a piece of me that afternoon and now he was the only person who could make me whole again.

I chastised myself for acting like such a teenager. I hadn't been this caught up on a boy since...

My thought was interrupted by my own clumsiness. I tripped on my bedroom carpet and face planted right into the bed. As a result, my towel unraveled and I was left exposed.

If only Vern were here...

I slapped my own head. This was getting out of hand.

Resolved to shove him to the furthest recesses of my mind, I got dressed into something comfortable. After all, I didn't have a job to go to.

Speaking of which...

I shuffled over to my laptop and turned it on. It took a while to boot up. I was due for a new one soon but I had a lot more pressing things to worry about like my electricity bill, for example. I could mentally picture the stack of unopened mails on the kitchen table. I knew running from my responsibilities was not the proper thing to do but honestly, I was at the end of my rope. When my severance package ran out so did my money. Now, I was scrambling to find a job and my experience as a bank manager wasn't getting me much of anything.

"You've got mail!"

The nostalgic greeting from my inbox did little to cheer me up. With my breath held, I clicked on the envelope icon. The subject lines were not very promising.

Rejection after rejection.

My shoulders sagged.

If I didn't find a job, I'd be out of a home.

Sure, my friend, Becky would let me couch surf at her place, but it wasn't a permanent solution. I couldn't live off her generosity for the rest of my life.

Frustrated, I slammed my laptop shut. With all my pent-up energy, all I could do was pace around like a cornered animal.

What was I supposed to do?

I went to the kitchen to get a snack but instead of finding comfort, I found only emptiness. Without the funds to go grocery shopping, I was surviving off of ramen noodles and scrambled eggs. Both options were starting to get really sickening.

Maybe I should have accepted Vern's offer to head down to The Shoppe...

"That's it," I said aloud. "I'm going to see him again. It's crazy, but I have to." With this thought in mind, I changed into some jeans and a tight-fitting tank top. Was I trying to impress him by wearing such form-fitting clothing? To be honest, I wasn't sure. All I knew was that I would lose my mind if I stayed in that house another minute.

I grabbed my bag and headed for the door.

The second I stepped onto the porch, I was bombarded by bright sunlight. I stopped and checked my phone for the time. It was only four. The club probably didn't open for a couple more hours.

I huffed. Now, what was I supposed to do?

With no other choice, I marched back inside and started filling out a few more job applications. At this point, I was applying to anything and everything. I even went so low as to apply to work for the local trash facility.

Each time I sent one off, I whispered a silent little prayer. Right now, I needed all the help I could get or I'd be living inside a cardboard box underneath the bridge.

And I just couldn't let that happen.

Chapter 3 Vern

The night was a typical one.

As always, a live rock band was playing on stage. They had succeeded in getting some people off their chairs and moving but, for the most part, people cradled their drinks and stared into the distance.

Humans had strange habits, that's for sure. They were so easily intoxicated and yet, they insisted on it. Sometimes, it even looked like they enjoyed it despite the agony it brought them the morning after.

"What are you daydreaming about?" Came a familiar voice.

I looked up and saw Lyle sitting at the counter. Strange. He never came to my neck of the woods unless something was troubling him. "What's up?" I asked.

"Nothing."

I poured him a drink. "Oh, come now! We're mating partners, you can't lie to me."

"Don't say that so loudly," Lyle hissed. "Someone might get the wrong idea."

"What? That we're gay?" I laughed and motioned to the overflowing tip jar. "I've had almost every girl in this place hit on me. Even if I were gay, I don't think they would care all that much."

Lyle growled.

"Someone's in a bad mood."

"Something's been bugging me but I don't know what. It's like an itch I can't scratch. It keeps burning just underneath the skin –"

"You might want to have that checked out –"

Lyle smashed his glass into the counter, nearly shattering it. His loss of temper caused his eyes to slit.

"Your dragon is showing," I teased. I was definitely pushing my luck but sometimes it was just too much fun to toy with him. He was always so serious all the time. He really needed to lighten up.

"I don't know why I bother to come here," Lyle muttered underneath his breath.

"Because, like it or not, I'm the person – or should I say dragon – that you trust the most and when something is bothering you, you like to talk about it."

Lyle rose from his seat and left without a single word more. Sometimes, his alpha nature made him so unapproachable. A lot of people would consider him an asshole, but I've known him all my life and he's much more than that. It just takes quite a bit to warm up to the guy.

Now left alone, I took to cleaning the counters. There wasn't much my rag could do to get rid of the years of grime but I certainly tried my best.

I was really starting to break a sweat when Ari walked through the doors. She stopped and looked around, wide-eyed like a deer caught in headlights. It was pretty obvious that she wasn't the sort of girl who came here often. I liked that. In a way, it was almost like I could smell her innocence wafting through the air but realistically it was probably some stud's overactive cologne.

She finally got her bearings and approached the bar. I flashed her a smile. "I didn't think I would see you so soon. This is such a lovely surprise."

"What can I say? You made quite the impression."

"Good or bad?" I asked. I tried to be subtle about it, but I couldn't help myself from peeking at her cleavage. I mean, you can't blame me. It was on display for all to see!

Luckily, she didn't catch me in the act and luckily, I had the bar to hide my obvious excitement.

"Honestly, I'm not sure yet."

"I'll take that as a good thing. At least I'm not on your shit list yet."

"Not yet."

"So, what will it be?" I asked.

"What's your cheapest drink? I'll have that."

"Cheapest, hmm?" I rubbed my chin as if deep in contemplation. "Well, we have this draft beer that tastes like piss..."

She screwed up her face with disgust. "And how, exactly would you know what piss tastes like?"

"Let's not talk about it." I leaned forward. "Because if we do, I'll be forced to kill you."

Ari laughed. It was a pleasant sort of sound that filled me with happiness. In all my years, I had never heard anything quite like it.

"How about this? I'll buy you a drink."

"Not going to happen. You've already hit on me enough for one day. I don't need you getting the wrong idea." I could tell she was the stubborn type. She had even crossed her arms over her chest which only obscured my wonderful view.

"There has to be a reason you came over to visit me."

"Maybe I just wanted a drink," she returned, her voice as clipped as she could make it but I could see the blush creeping behind her skin.

"Sure, sure. But I doubt you came here for the draft beer." I took one good look at her, eyes narrowing in scrutiny. "If you ask me, you're a vodka and Sprite kind of girl."

"How did you know...?" she stammered.

"I'm a bartender. It's my job to know these things." As I spoke, I whipped up her beverage and placed it on a coaster before sliding it in her direction. It stopped right in front of her.

"Whoa... that's a pretty neat trick."

"I like to think so." I grinned. "And so do my adoring fans."

"Hmm?"

To make up for the free drink, I took the money from my tip jar and placed it in the register.

"Oh..." It was like she was in a balloon and someone had just poked her with a needle. "I bet you have a lot of girls in here who think you're pretty cute."

"But there's only one girl whose opinion matters right now." I dropped my voice to a husky whisper, "and I believe her name is Ari."

This time, her cheeks became bright red. "I'm not falling for it. There are plenty of girls in here that are way more attractive than I could ever hope to be."

Without warning, I cupped her chin in my hand. "Shh," I said. "I don't want you talking about yourself like that. You're a gorgeous woman and there's really no need for you to put yourself down."

Now, her whole face was the color of a cherry tomato. It was incredibly cute. If I were a younger dragon, I would have kissed her right then and there. But with age, I had learned that to do such a thing usually resulted in a slap to the face. Human women didn't appreciate sudden shows of affection very much.

"Anyway, what's the problem?"

"Problem?" She asked.

"You look like you've got something weighing on your shoulders and as a bartender, I'm pretty much a certified therapist."

"What makes you think I would tell you my problems?" She sipped on her vodka to avoid looking me in the eye. "I don't even know you."

"All the better. I'm a stranger. What does it matter if I judge you?" I tossed my rag over my shoulder. "It's just an offer. You don't have to tell me a thing, but I can promise you that it'll make you feel better."

She nibbled her bottom lip in contemplation. "You promise not to judge?"

"Cross my heart and hope to die."

She downed the rest of her drink, as if to muster courage. Whatever was bugging her – it was serious. My body tightened like it wanted to spring into action. My arms yearned to hold her – to soothe her. I imagined myself whispering sweet nothings into her ear and telling her everything would be okay.

Now, I'll admit, I've flirted with my fair share of women. Some of them might even call me a playboy. But in all my time, I had never felt this way before. There was something about this woman that instilled in me a strength I didn't know I had.

"Well, about eight months ago, the bank I worked for had to cut some of its staff. They decided I needed to go. So, they gave me a severance package but it ended about two months ago. In all that time, I haven't been able to find myself a job. So, suffice to say, I'm a little strapped for cash."

I listened to her story and watched as she ran her finger along the rim of her now empty glass. I refilled it for her before resting a hand on her shoulder. "I have one of two options for you."

Ari raised an eyebrow in my direction.

"One, you could work here."

"At the bar?" She looked around. "I don't really know if it's my sort of work environment. Besides, I don't have much experience mixing drinks."

"Don't take this the wrong way but I figured as much. And, not to mention, you're a klutz. They definitely wouldn't want to hire someone who might break all the expensive bottles."

"Hey!" She protested, hand on her hip. By doing so, she drew my attention to that particular part of her body. A surge of excitement ravaged my body. She had the perfect hourglass body. Mmm. And the worst part? I don't even think she was aware of how damned sexy she was. "I'm not that clumsy."

I blinked. "Huh?"

"Forget it. What's the second option?"

"My roommate." I paused, slightly hesitant to give this gorgeous girl away to Lyle. I knew his nature and I didn't want Ari to get hurt by his crudeness. But, at the end of the day, us dragons needed to be in agreement before mating someone. If I liked Ari, then Lyle had to like her too. Since he wasn't one for dates, this was my best way of getting them inside the same room together. "He needs a personal assistant and I think you're just his type."

"Just his type...?" She repeated. "What does that mean?"

"Sorry, that came out a bit wrong." I held out my hands in apology. "What I mean is –" Luckily, my need for an explanation was interrupted by a bunch of burly men sitting down at the bar. I tended to them despite the jealousy that coursed through my veins when they looked over at Ari. One man, in particular, had no qualms about making his intentions very clear.

To block his view of her, I grabbed a rack of cups and placed them on the counter. I pretended I was very busy cleaning them even though they were already spotless. Only then did I return to Ari. "So, yeah, as I was saying, my roommate needs a personal assistant."

She frowned. "I mean, I appreciate the offer but I really don't have any experience with secretary work."

"Why don't you send him a resume anyway? It won't hurt. Besides, I'll put in a good word for you." I fished through my wallet and pulled out one of Lyle's business cards. It was dogged eared in all four corners and the ink was a little faded. "Sorry, they've been in here a while."

"I can tell." Nonetheless, she took the card and tucked it into her purse. "In any case, why are you doing this for me? I mean, you don't really know who I am. Why would you stick out your neck for me?"

I smiled and leaned forward so only she could hear my voice. "Because I have kryptonite for cute girls."

She laughed. "Where'd you learn that pick-up line, Casanova?" With that, she jumped down from her stool and slung her purse over her shoulder. "I think that's my cue to leave."

"Would you mind texting me when you get home?"

"Why?" She asked.

"Because I'd just like to know whether you got there safe and sound. I swear, I'm not trying to make a move."

"Oh, alright." She handed over her phone. "Do you mind punching in your number. The one you wrote on my arm washed away after I showered."

"Sure thing," I answered but my mind was already far, far away. I imagined her naked body standing underneath a stream of hot water. Oh, what a wonderful sight. "There you go. And if you'd like to call me sometime –"

"Bye!" She cut me off with a wave.

And the last I saw of her was that cute little ass swaying from side to side.

Chapter 4 Ari

A few days later.

I crashed on the couch, about to turn on an afternoon sitcom when my phone started to buzz. I snatched it up from the coffee table and saw System Safe on the caller ID.

My heart quickened. Could it be that Vern had actually landed me a job?

The phone continued to ring.

In my daze, I nearly forgot to answer it. Thankfully, I caught it at the last second. "Hello?" My voice was ragged and I silently reprimanded myself for not being able to keep myself under control.

"Is this Miss Ari Greene?"

"Y-Yes." Again, my voice wavered.

"I would like to inform you that Mr. Stokes has decided to bring you in for an interview. He has requested to see you tomorrow morning at nine. Are you available during this time?"

"Yes!" I jumped off the couch with excitement. "I'll be there."

"Good. I would just like to remind you to bring a copy of your resume and on behalf of the System Safe team, we wish you the best of luck."

"Thank you." This time, I spoke with a whisper.

The call ended and I was greeted with the dial tone. A wave of disbelief washed over me. After almost a year of little to no luck, I finally had the opportunity I needed. Perhaps I did not have the experience they were looking for but I would make damn sure that they understood I was the best woman for the job. I would work my ass off if I needed to.

When the elation faded away, a thought dawned on me: What was I going to wear? I rushed to my closet and pulled back the doors. At first glance, everything looked horrible drab. I shifted the hangers from one side to the other, searching for anything that might deem business professional. After all, I wanted these people to like me especially since Vern had recommended me. I didn't want to make him look bad.

I groaned. There was nothing – nothing.

After glancing out my window, I groaned even louder. It was raining cats and dogs out there, but I didn't have much of a choice. If I didn't get an outfit today, then I would be showing up to my interview in a pair of ripped skinny jeans. They would probably end up kicking me out at the front door.

So, I dawned my raincoat and hopped on the bus. Once I reached Main St. I made a bee-line for my favorite thrift store. At one point in my life, I would have been embarrassed to shop at such a place but right now, I couldn't complain. The boutiques that had once been my stomping grounds were out of the question.

A clap of thunder echoed through the clouds. The rain thickened. To avoid the downpour, I raced across the street. I'll admit, I didn't quite look both ways but this red car was definitely speeding.

The tires screeched against the asphalt as the car came to an abrupt halt.

My heart leaped to my throat as I saw my life flash before my eyes. To brace myself, I rested a hand against the hood. It was warm – much warmer than the rain that kept crashing down all around me.

I looked up, expecting to see a driver but the windows were so tinted that I couldn't see a thing. Still, a shiver crept through my spine. Whoever was behind that steering wheel seemed to stare a hole into my soul. Intimidated by the invisible stare, I stepped aside.

As soon as the road was clear, the car peeled away. I had just enough time to glance at the license plate number. I considered calling it in for reckless driving but in all honesty, what good would that do? Someone with that much money probably had a few friends in the force.

"Ma'am, are you okay?" asked a concerned bystander.

"Yes, I'm fine," I answered despite the fact that I had nearly been killed.

I didn't wait for further questions. It was getting cold and I didn't want to stand in the rain any longer. So, without further delay, I stowed into the thrift shop.

It was surprisingly warm. The musty smell of old books and vintage items seemed to grow stronger with the heat. I breathed it in.

"Ari!" came a familiar voice.

I turned and saw my best friend standing at the cash register. "Hey, Becky."

"Why didn't you tell me you were coming over?"

"Kind of a spur of the moment thing," I said. "I finally got a job interview and now I'm in desperate need of something to wear."

"I've got you covered," Becky said with a grin. "We just got some new stuff and I think some of it is actually in your size."

I followed her to the back where she circled around a specific rack looking like a hawk about to swoop down on its helpless prey.

"Ah! Here it is!" She said as she grabbed a blazer and held it against my body. "I think that would do quite nicely. Don't you agree?"

"I can't quite see it. Let me try some of this stuff on and then I'll tell you what I think."

She nodded and unlocked one of the fitting rooms for me.

I walked inside and hung up the clothes she had picked out for me. When I turned around to close the door, there she was again with another bundle. "I thought you might like these as well. They're on markdown but they're still pretty good."

"Jeez, Becky, I didn't come here to try out the entire store."

She laughed. "Sorry, I just got a little carried away. I'll leave you alone. If you need anything, I'll be in the front."

"Thank you." I waited for her to walk away before finally locking the door.

I leaned against it and studied the pile of clothing. Many of the pieces had a funny smell to them and others were horribly discolored.

How had my life gotten this low so quickly? I was well on my way to becoming an executive manager when wham, I was laid off. I never saw it coming. I thought I was an essential part of the staff but the higher-ups clearly didn't think the same.

With a sigh, I pushed away these depressing thoughts from my mind and dawned some of the cleanest looking clothing. The first sweater was much too itchy for me to stand and the blouse I tried on after that was pretty much see through.

I didn't fare much better in the pants department. Some were baggy while others didn't fit around the waist.

Maybe it wasn't the clothes. Maybe it was me.

I stood in front of the mirror and frowned. I always thought myself weirdly shaped. My hips were much too big and my chest not big enough. For this reason, clothes never quite hugged my body the same way they did with other girls. Becky had once told me that I didn't know how to properly dress for my body type but I think that was just her being nice.

Tears welled up in my eyes but I didn't dare shed them. Sure, my life might be in the hole but I wasn't going to get anywhere with self-pity. So, I held up my head and rummaged through the various outfits until I found something I liked.

It wasn't the greatest but it would have to do.

As I picked them up, I had a little moment of remembrance for all the pantsuits I had once owned. They were one of the first things I sold in hopes of making end's meet. Now I seriously regretted getting rid of them all. But hey, a girl has got to eat.

"All set?" Becky asked with a smile.

"I think so," I said as I pulled out my wallet.

She scanned the few articles of clothing. I held my breath as I saw the number on the screen getting higher and higher. I feared I wouldn't have enough to cover it.

"Alright, that'll be..." she paused and pressed a button that dinged rather loudly. Abruptly, the amount was slashed by nearly eighty percent.

I released the breath I had been holding.

"Are you okay?"

"Fine." I handed over the cash.

"Good luck with the interview! I hope you get the job." She offered one of her bright smiles as I grabbed my bag.

"Thanks, Becky. I'll keep you updated."

"Please do!"

With that, I braved the rain once more. This time, I was spared the red Ferrari.

Chapter 5 Lyle

The following day. 8:30 A.M.

My coffee was yet to work its magic. It was warm within my system but that was the extent of it. This was what happened whenever I allowed my current secretary to handle my caffeine. She had a penchant for forgetting about my double shot of espresso.

I pinched the bridge of my nose in frustration before pouring it out in favor of a new one. As the coffee machine grinded up the beans, the thick aroma wafted into the air and coated my office with its richness. That smell was one of the few things that could bring a smile to my face.

As I waited, I walked over to my desk and checked my itinerary for the day.

Ah, that's right. I had an interview with a Miss Greene this morning. Despite her lack of qualifications, Vern had insisted I give her a chance. If I didn't know any better, I would have guessed he was smitten with her. Which means –

My thoughts were interrupted by a knock. "Come in," I called.

Susan stepped inside. "Miss Greene has arrived. Would you like me to send her in or have her wait until nine?"

"Send her in," I said.

Susan hastened out of the room.

As the door came to a close, the coffee machine started up. I waited impatiently for my mug to fill. It seemed to take an eternity but when it was done and I was finally able to have a sip, I was glad for the wait. This was leaps and bounds better than the dirty water I was drinking before.

I closed my eyes and savored the taste.

Just then, there came another knock. This time, I forfeited my coffee to the countertop and walked over to answer the door myself. I grabbed the handle and turned it.

I can tell you that I was not expecting the woman I saw before me. "Ari?" I blurted, losing sight of myself.

Her eyes widened. No doubt she recognized who I was. "Lyle..." She whispered with an air of disbelief. "Y-You're the CEO of this place?" She stammered and shifted from foot to foot.

I ran my fingers through my hair to keep from growing. Why hadn't Vern warned her? Then again, how would he have known? He was off in Europe at the time. "Please, come inside and we can start our interview."

She lingered by the doorway. "You know, I don't think this is such a good idea. I appreciate the offer, I really do –"

"Sit." My voice held an edge to it that I hadn't intended.

She gulped but nonetheless, followed my command by walking over to one of the couches. When she went to sit down, she sunk into the cushions. The unexpectedness of it threw her off balance and her struggle to right herself nearly resulted in her flashing me. Quickly, she tugged on the hem of her skirt and pulled it down the length of her skirt.

My blood boiled with desire. It seemed she had the same effect on me now as she did back then. But what did it matter? Ari Greene was off limits. Years ago, my dream of being with her had been crushed by the clan elder when he told that she had been claimed by the Aetos – our sworn enemies.

To have anything romantic with her would mean starting an all-out war and I just couldn't jeopardize the safety of my people that way. But there was nothing against hiring her as an employee.

As subtly as I could, I scanned her over for any markings. From what I could tell, she hadn't mated yet. What were they waiting for?

"Uh..." Ari spoke up.

"Right." I cleared my throat and cleared my mind of any unnecessary thoughts. Right now, I was here to talk about business. "Vern told me you were looking for a job."

She nodded and a strand of her hair came loose from the bun that sat atop her head. She pinned it behind her ear, drawing attention to her exposed neck. Oh, how I wanted to sink my teeth into her sensitive skin and hear her moan my name.

"Yes." She paused to wet her lips.

At this point, I was convinced she was doing this on purpose. That Aetos had sent her here to tempt me. Well, I wasn't going to fall for it. "What has been your experience since our time working together?"

"You mean since Sim's Ice Cream Shop?"

"Yes."

"Well, I became a bank teller and worked my way up the ranks until I became a manager." As she spoke, she pulled out a clean sheet of paper from a folder I hadn't noticed. "This is my resume if you want to take a look."

"Don't bother," I said. "I've already taken a look and as far as I'm concerned, you aren't qualified for this job." I reached over and grabbed a thick stack of applications from my desk. "There are dozens of people looking to snag this job. Why should I give it to you?" I dropped the applications on the table.

Slam!

Ari flinched and recoiled back.

"And if your work ethic is anything like it used to be then, I would only be wasting my time hiring you."

Abruptly, Ari rose to her feet. By her sides, her hands had tightened into fists and they were shaking like she wanted to punch something. "I see that you're as much of a jerk as you used to be when we were teenagers! I never understood why you hated me so much but I guess that doesn't matter. I won't be getting this job. You've made that clear. So, I'm not going to sit here and let you toy with me as you used to all those years ago." Her anger caused her chest to rise and fall in an erratic manner.

Over the years, she had filled out her form quite nicely. I yearned to push her against the wall and have my way with her. Even her damned scent was intoxicating. My nostrils flared with the need to breathe it in.

"I'm done here." She snapped before turning on her heels. She managed a few steps before the tip of her shoe scuffed the floor. She stumbled and accidentally crashed into a glass table. The diorama I had on display there was pushed off the edge where it shattered into a million pieces.

Ari braced herself against the glass table looking like a deer caught in headlights.

In any other situation, I would have been fuming but the sight of her bent over like that...

I crossed the room and grabbed her by the arm, whipping her around. "Are you alright?" My voice came out as a rough whisper. Her body was impossibly close to mine and it took every inch of my willpower to keep my raging hormones in check. I wanted to pounce on her right then and there but to do so would be horribly selfish of me. I couldn't do that to my clan. As one of the alphas, it was my duty to protect them. There would be other girls.

"Y-Yes," she answered. "I think so." She looked down at the mess she had created. "I am horribly sorry about that. Is there any way I can remedy it? Glue maybe..."

"Don't bother wasting your time." I sighed. "I've already closed the deal for that project anyway." I narrowed my eyes to study hers. "Are you sure you're okay? Maybe you should sit down and have something to drink in case you're feeling dizzy."

She shook her head. "No, no. I'm not dizzy at all. I only tripped." She released herself from my hold and bent down to gather up some of the debris.

I was forced to bite the inside of my cheek to keep my thoughts from wandering. The fabric of her skirt was tight against her ass and I could barely stand it. Then, she dropped to her hands and knees. She was practically begging me to do something.

To get her to stop, I cleared my throat. "I'll have my janitor handle it. I believe he's better equipped."

Ari blushed. "Right." She dusted off her knees and avoided looking me in the eye.

"Well, I believe we are done here. Let me walk you to the door." I took her hand and held it in a firm grip. A surge of energy made its way along my arm. The hairs on the nape of my neck stood on edge and I swear my eyes shifted as my dragon side became desperate for freedom.

I had no doubt in my mind that this woman was meant to be my mate and yet, she was out of my grasp.

"You'll hear from us in a few days," I said.

"Thank you."

Maybe I couldn't have her as a mate but I wasn't going to let her out of my sights again. Even if she ended up being the worse personal assistant on the planet, at least she would be mine.

Chapter 6 Ari

The following day.

Becky's house always smelled like freshly baked cookies. My stomach growled just thinking of the gooey treats and the delicious chocolate chips she packed into every batch.

"You came just in time," Becky said with a smile as she reached into her oven and pulled out a tray.

"At this rate, you should consider opening up your own bakery. People would pay good money for these things." As I reached forward to grab one, she slapped my hand away. "Ouch!"

"They're hot!" She chided. "I don't want you burning yourself."

I groaned, "Does that mean I have to wait for them to cool?"

Becky clicked her tongue against the roof of her mouth. "Patience is a virtue."

"Yeah, well, after yesterday I'm not in the best of moods." I slumped into a nearby chair and fiddles with the salt n' pepper shakers.

"I was hoping you would tell me about that." She took off her apron and hung it up on a peg. Becky was one of those super organized types. Every single thing in her home had its place. "So, it didn't go well, then?"

"Not at all." I huffed. "You won't even believe who the CEO happens to be."

"Who?"

"Lyle. Fucking Lyle." His name was enough to bring the taste of disgust to my mouth. "I thought I was done with him when I quit the ice cream parlor." Unable to contain the pent-up frustration welling up inside of me, I got up and paced the length of her kitchen. "And he's just as a much of a jerk as he was back then."

"He didn't do anything to you, did he?" Becky asked with a frown. "I mean, did he say anything nasty?"

"He didn't cuss me out or anything but he wasn't exactly pleasant to talk to." I stopped and opened up her back door. A refreshing breeze rolled in, cooling some of the heat from my cheats. "Why does he have to be such an arrogant asshole? He acts like he owns the entire world but last time I checked, no one crowned him king."

She got up and retrieved a couple of plates from the china cabinet. "Are you sure this has nothing to do with the fact that you used to like him?"

I whipped around so fast that my vision blurred. "I did not like that guy."

"Oh yeah?" She raised an eyebrow. "I think you're lying."

"I'm not lying. Why would I ever like that guy? He doesn't know the first thing about manners. All he cares about is himself."

"I don't know..." she taunted. "I used to remember you staring at him all the time. And you have to admit that he was pretty damn cute."

I snatched up a cookie and tore into it. "Well, either way, I'm not taking the job."

"I thought you really needed one."

"I do, but..."

"You're going to let this guy get in your way?" She asked. "Aren't you just letting him win that way?"

I sighed and joined her at the table. "I guess you're right but I doubt he would even want to hire me. He said I wasn't qualified and then he showed me this big ol' stack of papers from all the other applicants. Realistically, I don't stand a chance."

"I wouldn't be so sure." She said. "Back when we were teenagers, he used to stare at you too."

Chapter 7 Vern

The following morning.

I searched the park, looking for her. So far, I hadn't spotted her yet.

The power walkers passed me for the third time. Geraldine didn't forget to offer a scandalous little wink as she went by. I winked back and heard her giggle all the way down the path.

Perhaps Ari wasn't planning on jogging today. But it was such a beautiful day. It almost seemed like a crime to be cooped up inside.

I walked over to the water fountain and had myself a drink. When I looked up, there she was. "Geraldine tipped me off that you were waiting for me,"she said with her arms crossed against her chest. "Do you make it a habit of stalking girls you've only just met?"

"Stalking? I hardly consider this stalking. Wait until I start hiding in your shrubbery."

Her eyes widened. "Wait, you're not actually going to do that, are you?"

"Of course..." I trailed off. "...not." I grinned. "What kind of hooligan do you take me for?"

"I don't know. You look like a pretty big one to me."

I feigned offense. "I'll have you know that I work out five times a week!"

"Do you now?" I didn't miss the sweep of her eyes over my body. Clearly, I had her interested. Good. "Anyway, have you eaten lunch yet?"

"It's only eleven."

"Yeah, well, I thought we could have ourselves a little picnic before we get super sweaty. I made cream cheese and cucumber sandwiches."

Ari furrowed her brows together. "You made what now?"

"Cream cheese and cucumber sandwiches."

"What kind of combination is that?" She shook her head.

"Plenty of people eat them. It's quite common in England. They have them with their afternoon tea."

"But we're not in England. Around here most people eat peanut butter and jelly sandwiches."

I screwed up my face. "I hate jelly."

"That's it. You must be an alien." She threw her hands into the air and said, "And I don't think I can enjoy a picnic with an alien."

"Won't you at least try?" I grabbed her by the arm and towed her toward the shade of the closest tree. "I promise you will not regret it."

Once we were by the tree, I removed a blanket from the basket and laid it down.

"You really thought this through, didn't you?"

"It takes a fair bit of work and consideration to impress a girl, especially one as pretty as you." I flashed her a smile before unpacking our lunch.

She avoided looking directly at me as she sat down, legs crossed one of the other. Her cheeks were a lovely shade of pink. It seemed she was the sort of girl who was prone to blushing. Man, could this girl get any cuter?

"You know, these aren't so bad," she said as she nibbled on the end of a sandwich. "But still a fairly weird combination."

I leaned back and looked up at the clouds. "So, how did the interview go? I asked my roommate about it but he's not exactly one for conversations."

"How do you stand living with that guy? I'm sorry but he's a pretty big jerk," she said, lying down beside me. The skin of our arms rubbed together. A tingling sensation crawled into my muscles and invigorated them with a newfound strength. This was my dragon speaking, telling me that I had to protect this woman at all times.

"Well, he's not home very often. Most of the time, he's working and when he's not working, he's reading and you wouldn't want to disturb him when he's reading."

"I wouldn't peg him as a book worm."

"Neither would most people." I agreed as I sat up and reached across her to grab the thermos. By doing so, I was nearly laying on top of her. Time seemed to stop as our faces came dangerously close. The warmth of her breath teased the top of my lips, tempting me to make a move. But this was Lyle's girl. To have her without his consent would be a crime against my alpha. And pity on those that deny their alpha.

I pulled away and poured us both some iced tea. "Here."

"Thanks." She took a sip and gazed into the distance.

I admired her out of the corner of my eye, wondering what was going on in that head of hers. "It's a beautiful day, isn't it?"

"Yes, it is. I wouldn't mind sitting underneath this tree all day long."

"Does that mean you're finally starting to enjoy my company?"

"I wouldn't go that far –" Her words were interrupted by a rogue soccer ball flying her way. She screamed and braced herself but didn't think to get out of the way. Luckily, I stuck out my hand at just the right moment, blocking its path.

The palm of my hand stung with the impact but I didn't mind it so long as Ari's beautiful face was safe and sound.

"Sorry!" A kid wearing a jersey grabbed his ball and ran off.

Ari breathed a sigh of relief. "Phew. That was a close one." She looked over at me. "Those are some killer reflexes you got there. Are you sure you're not some kind of alien?"

I laughed. "That's some way you have of thanking me. I should be insulted that you keep thinking I'm some sort of slimy alien."

"That's not –"

I reached forward and cupped her cheek against my hand. It must have taken her by surprise because she stopped talking. "I'm just glad you're okay." Again, her lips tempted me with their silkiness. It was torture to keep my distance.

"Right…" she whispered as if in a daze. Slowly, she leaned forward, eyes shut.

I dropped my hand and reached into my back pocket. "Now that you owe me a favor, I think it's a good time to ask you."

"Ask me what?" She raised an eyebrow in question.

"Well, you see, Lyle invited me to this gala. It's hosted by the company. It's sort of this annual thing they have every year –"

"Hence, annual," she interjected with a sly grin.

"Yeah, right." I didn't know why but there were beads of sweat running down the back of my neck. I felt like a young dragon asking out a girl for the first time. "Well, he got me two tickets in case I wanted to bring a date."

"And you want me to go with you?"

"Only if you want to, that is. I would never make you go but I can promise you that it's actually a lot of fun. And, there's a lot of food."

She laughed. "If there's any cream cheese and cucumber sandwiches then you can count me in."

"And I know you don't like my roommate very much but I figured this would be a good opportunity for you to get his attention."

"What do you mean?"

"The green-eyed monster."

"You want to make your own roommate jealous? Why?"

I tore at some grass and sprinkled it on the blanket. "Because he always gets what he wants. It's about time I get what I want."

Chapter 8 Ari

I stood in front of my closet, desperately searching for something to wear. After spending all my spare cash on business attire, I was forced to choose from what I already owned. I clicked my tongue against the roof of my mouth, disappointed by my selection.

"Jeez..." I groaned aloud as I pulled out a sequin mini skirt. When did I think it was okay to wear such a dastardly thing?

How was I supposed to make Lyle jealous when I would most certainly arrive at this gala looking like a slob?

Why was I even trying so hard to make him jealous in the first place?

Because, deep down, you like him, came that voice in the back of my head.

I shook it away and kept searching. It was then that I heard a knock at the front door. My eyes widened with panic. Was that Vern already? I tightened the sash of my bathrobe. I hadn't even bothered to throw on underwear yet. With this thought, I dashed towards the dresser and grabbed the first pair I got my hands on. In my attempt to put them on, I fell, crashing onto the ground.

"What in the world...?" Becky was standing at the doorway to my bedroom, covering her eyes against my indecency. "Do you want to explain what you're doing right now."

My whole face felt like it was going to melt off with embarrassment. "Becky! I thought I told you to stop barging into my apartment!"

"Well, if you really want me to stop then you should really consider moving the location of your spare key where I can't find it." She peeked through her fingers. "Looking good, by the way."

"Becky!" I forced my robe shut and sprung to my feet. As a result, my panties fell back to the ground. I yanked them up my legs and huffed.

"Someone's a little wound up." Becky stepped forward when it was safe to do so.

"What are you doing here, anyway?"

"I figured you might need some help getting ready for this gala." She dropped a few garment bags onto my bed. "I picked these up from the shop. Consider it an early Christmas present."

"It's July."

She shrugged and unzipped the topmost bag. I expected it to be some gaudy prom dress but what she revealed surpassed my wildest expectations. It was a lovely shade of burgundy with an exposed back and subtle flowers stitched into the skirt. "Wow..."

"That's what I'm saying." Becky grinned. "I was tempted to keep it for myself but I think it would suit you much better. You have the body for it."

I didn't know whether to take her words as a compliment or a backhanded insult.

"Try it on!" she said, practically pushing me into the bathroom.

Thud.

Once the door was shut, I hung up the dress. It was even more beautiful in my bathroom's brightness. Small gemstones added a bit of sparkle.

I ran my fingers over the soft fabric. Sometimes I wondered how I had managed to snag a friend as good as Becky. She was always looking out for me.

Finally, I dropped my robe to the ground. The cool air caressed my sensitive skin, causing goosebumps to prickle along my breasts. I covered them with my hands. My nipples poked against my hands with excitement. That excitement wasn't due to the dress but the thought of what it might feel like to have Vern take it off my body.

I wanted to feel his hot breath against the side of my neck. Or better yet, the heat of his body pressed against mine as he reached around to take my breasts into his hands. Mmm, oh yes, that's what

I wanted. Consumed by this fantasy, I leaned against the sink, hips thrusting forward as if to greet an invisible lover.

"Is everything alright in there?" Becky tried the doorknob. The rattling startled me back into reality.

"Yes, just a minute," I answered. My cheeks were flushed with the thought of Vern. I washed it away with some cold tap water before dawning the dress.

It almost felt like it was made for me. The fabric had a bit of stretch to it which meant it hugged every part of my body but it was thick enough to conceal all those troubled areas.

Using the mirror, I tied the halter top around my neck. Doing so, my breasts were lifted and accentuated to the perfect degree. In fact, it was perhaps a little more revealing than I was comfortable with but, at the same time, I had to admit that it looked pretty damn good.

I did a little twirl so I could get a better view of my backside. Damn.

"Did you fall in or something?" Becky called through the door.

With a wild grin, I unlocked it and posed.

"Whoa…"

"You're a genius," I said. "I've never looked this good."

She clapped her hands together. "And I'm not even done with you yet. I still have to do your make-up and hair."

"Jeez. This isn't my wedding, you know."

She took me by the shoulders and sat me down in front of my vanity. "I decided to do a little research and this gala is one of the biggest events in town. Anyone who is anyone is going to be there."

"So?"

"So?" She repeated. "This is your chance to prove to Lyle that you're not the dorky girl you used to be."

"Hey!"

"No offense babe but you used to wear tie-dye shirts." Becky sorted through my cosmetics. "Tonight, you're going to show him exactly what he's missing out on."

While it was true that I wanted to get my revenge, I didn't know if it was worth all the trouble. It didn't matter what I did, Lyle was never going to notice me. He would always think he was better than me. But, then again, there was nothing stopping me from using all this glitz and glam to impress Vern. He would never know what hit him.

"I've seen that look in your eye before. What are you thinking?"

"I'm thinking, screw Lyle. He isn't worth my time."

"Oh?"

"But Vern..."

"You mean that guy who keeps stalking you in the park?" Becky paused and considered the eyeshadow palette in her hands. "You haven't talked about it much but, by the looks of it, you're smitten."

"I didn't think so at first. He's a little odd but I think I like it. He's different."

"So long as he makes you happy then I'm happy too." Becky handed me a tube of lipstick. "Try that on for me. I think it'll match the dress quite nicely.

I turned to look in the mirror. When I saw my reflection, I froze in place. I could barely recognize myself. "How did you learn how to do this?"

"I've been doing it as a side gig at my local saloon. Turns out I'm pretty good at it," she said with a smile. I was about to touch my face when she slapped my hands away. "Don't you dare."

"Sorry," I mumbled. Before I could get myself into further trouble, I applied the lipstick. It really completed the look.

"Knock 'em dead tonight, you hear me?"

"Oh, I don't think that'll be a problem," I said with a grin, my self-confidence hitting through the roof.

Chapter 9 Ari

"Well, I should get going. I've got a cat to feed."

"Thank you so much for coming over and helping me out," I said as I encased her in a tight, rib-crushing hug.

"Hug me any tighter and you'll lose your best friend," she groaned in a dramatic wheeze.

I eased my grip and chuckled. "Sorry."

"And be careful." She circled behind me and gave the neck straps a soft tug. "It wouldn't take much to undo these. I would hate for you to have a wardrobe malfunction." She was already packing up her things when she looked up and caught my eye. "Unless, of course, that's your intention."

"No!" I said in my defense. "Did you really think I'd want to flash a whole room of people?"

"Maybe not a whole room but someone in particular." Her lips curled into a knowing smirk. "And I think his name is Vern."

"Don't be ridiculous. I barely know the guy. I wouldn't fall into bed that quickly."

She shrugged. "I don't know. Sometimes these sorts of things just happen and you can't stop it when the temperature of the room starts to rise higher and higher."

"Stop it," I grumbled.

"Alright, alright. I think I've teased you enough for one night." She held up her hands in her innocence. "But I want to hear all about it tomorrow."

"Okay." I agreed.

"I'll be awaiting that phone call," she said as she carried the unused garments to the front door.

I waved her off and watched as her car cruised down the street. It disappeared around the bend just as a pair of headlights shone in my direction. I was blinded by their brightness. I held up an arm against my eyes to shield them but even so, I wasn't able to see past the light.

It got brighter and brighter as the car made its way down the street. I expected it to keep going but it pulled into my driveway. Only then did the headlights become dim.

I blinked and to my surprise, Vern was sitting behind the wheel of a shiny new Jaguar. The sleek black paint nearly blended into the night.

My jaw hung ajar as he emerged wearing a fitted suit. The satin lapels and cuff links really screamed luxury.

"My, my, you look lovely," he said with a voice as smooth as whiskey.

"Wait." I shook my head. "You can't possibly be the same guy."

He laughed.

"I thought you were a bartender."

"I am."

"Then how on Earth can you afford all this?" I asked as I continued to stare at my date. I really hadn't expected him to look this attractive. With his dark hair swept back and his facial hair gone, he looked like some sort of movie star.

"Let's just say I'm good with money." He took my hand and kissed my knuckles. "Of course, if you'd prefer, I change into my jogging outfit, I can do that too."

"No!" I shook my head a little too hard and a strand of hair came undone from the bun that sat atop of my head. It framed the side of my face for a moment before Vern reached for it. His fingertips danced along my skin before he pinned the stray strand behind my ear.

A shiver went through my spine as our eyes locked together. I swear, my heart skipped a beat.

"Shall we? I wouldn't want us to be late."

"Y-Yeah." I stammered. "Just give me a moment." I rushed inside only to trip on the welcome mat. My ankle twisted and I was about to fall forward when I felt a strong arm wrap around my waist. A second later, I was pinned against Vern's chest.

I forgot how to breathe.

He smiled down at me. "Careful," was all that he said before he helped me regain my balance.

Get a grip, Ari, I told myself as I took a second to compose myself. Only then did I manage enough mobility to get my legs moving in the right direction. I grabbed my purse from my bedroom and was about to sling it over my shoulder when I reconsidered.

It was likely to get chilly at night so it was probably best if I brought along a light jacket. Becky had left one for me. I reached for it but it was already gone. "Huh?"

"Looking for this?" Vern was suddenly behind me, his words right against my ear.

I jumped slightly.

"Yeah," I said when I saw he was holding the jacket.

"Let me." He held it out so I could slip my arms through the sleeves. This guy really knew how to make a girl feel like royalty.

When it was on, he leaned down slightly and brushed his lips ever so gently against the skin of my neck.

I turned around and there he stood as if he hadn't kissed me at all. Had I imagined it? There was no way he could have moved that quickly.

"Are you ready?" He asked as he handed over my purse.

"Yeah, I think so."

"Good." He held out his arm so I could hold onto it. "I wouldn't want you to trip a second time." We were almost at the door when he stopped. "By the way, it's a pretty nice bedroom you've got here. It's almost a shame that we have this gala to go to."

A part of me wanted to suggest that we stay but I couldn't summon the courage. It just wasn't in me to be that kind of girl.

"Oh well, maybe another day," he said in a whisper that I guessed I wasn't supposed to hear. Nevertheless, I heard it, and they brought with them a vivid scene of Vern in bed with me. I had no doubt that underneath that suit and tie, he hid a wonderland of muscle. I could just envision myself running my hands all along them, feeling every bump and valley. "Ari?"

He said my name and I nearly moaned.

"Are you okay?"

Heat rose through my ears as I realized I had zoned off into a daydream. "Sorry."

He tipped his head in acknowledgment but did not say a word as he guided me over to his car. He opened the passenger-side door for me and made sure I was safely inside before he reached across and buckled me into place. By doing so, he had his body nearly pressed against mine. His scent invaded my nostrils. I breathed him in, growing intoxicated by the smell of his soap. It was subtle but pleasant. The hint of mint was a nice little touch.

"There we go," he said as he turned his head. It was so close to mine that all I needed to do was lean forward and...

He pulled away and my shoulders sagged with disappointment.

Through the windshield, I saw him round the car and get behind the wheel. A second later, we were speeding down the street, as he got on the highway. Instantly, I felt a rush of adrenaline as he pressed on the gas. I didn't need to look at the odometer to know we were going fast.

Out of the corner of my eye, I noticed him looking my way. What was he thinking? Did he like what he saw or was he regretting his choice of date?

Suddenly, I felt his hand on top of mine. "You really do look quite stunning." His hand then crept onto my exposed thigh. Under any other circumstance, I would have swatted him away but as a wave of excitement coursed through my veins, I responded by spreading my legs ever so slightly. What had gotten into me? I had never reacted this way before. It was like this man had unlocked some sort of primal instinct that had laid dormant inside of me. All I wanted to do was unleash it by pouncing on him and having my way with his sexy body.

My heart raced as his fingertips danced closer and closer to the thong I wore.

Then, rather abruptly, he pulled away and fiddled instead with the music. I nearly whimpered at the lack of intimacy. I didn't want him to stop. Hell, I wanted him to go all the way.

The air in the car was thick with my desires. I felt constrained by the seat belt that kept cutting my cleavage.

I was about to say something to break the silence that had settled between us when he stopped the car in front of a grand looking building. It was one of the seaside mansions - the one I had always dreamt of living in one day.

The gilded gates were open and well-dressed guests poured through them. Most of them wore masks.

"I didn't know this was a masquerade," I said, feeling horribly out of place.

"Don't worry." He responded as he reached into the back seat. "I got us a matching pair. I didn't want anyone to forget that you're with me." With a gentle touch, he helped me put it on.

"Thanks," I said as I returned the favor.

Once that was taken care of, he got out of the car and quickened to open my door. He offered me his hand, and as soon as I took it, he gripped me with a certain quality of strength that made me feel safe and sound.

Together, we made it up the long, winding driveway while valet parked his car.

"So, you've been to this even before?" I asked in a whisper. I couldn't help but notice all the gorgeous women. Surely, someone like Vern would have no trouble asking any number of them on a date and yet, he had chosen me of all people. It brought a smile to my face to know that I stood a chance against all these gorgeous women because I was gorgeous too.

"Right this way." A man dressed in a butler's outfit ushered us inside.

And man, was it gorgeous. I had never seen anything quite like it. The ceiling was vaulted and etched in the plaster were baroque-type swirls that gave the place an added level of class. A few of the columned archways were held up by winged women. Whoever had sculpted them sure was skilled.

I didn't have much time to admire them before I was whisked away into the ballroom. Vern held me firmly by the waist like he didn't want to run off and get lost. "Are you hungry?" He asked.

"Not particularly."

"Good because I didn't think I could have waited to dance with you."

In the blink of an eye, we were in the middle of the dancefloor. Vern had his hand on the small of my back while his other hand held mine at shoulder height.

Effortlessly, we glided across the floor, weaving in and out of the other couples. My dress fluttered around my ankles, catching the wind of my movements. The breeze it caused traveled along the length of my legs and settled between them. This only helped to highlight my current excitement. Were I to slip a hand underneath my thong, I would find a wetness unlike anything I had ever experienced before.

What was the man doing to me and why did I like it so much?

"Where did you learn to dance like this?" I asked as we eased into a slower pace.

"I took lessons."

"You're just full of surprises, aren't you?"

"One could say that." We spun around and I stumbled on his foot. He was quick to stabilize me by pressing me even closer to his body. At this point, we were practically glued together.

I could feel the beating of his heart against my own. They were beating as one as he carried me through the movements. In his capable hands, it almost felt like I was weightless.

He smiled down at me and his lips parted as he said something but I did not hear him. I had caught sight of Lyle. Even though he wore a mask, I knew it was him. He radiated a sort of power that made everyone give him a bit more space like he had an invisible forcefield around his body.

In his arms was a pencil-thin blonde with bouncing curls. Her breasts were on full display but to my amazement not once did he look down at them.

Even so, jealousy festered inside the pit of my stomach. I could feel it growing there like a stone gaining mass.

Her flirtatious laugh sliced through the room and penetrated through my eardrums.

Why was I so upset? Why did it matter who he danced with? I already had a handsome man by my side. I didn't need his arrogant ass.

And yet, deep down, I knew that was what I wanted.

Chapter 10 Lyle

The night was going just as planned. The decorations had been properly executed while the food expertly prepared. Each and every guest wore a smile. Champagne glasses clinked together as people indulged in merry conversation.

"May I?"

I turned and standing before me was Miss Belington, the daughter of one of my biggest investors. It was no secret that she fancied me but, in all honesty, I thought her rather dull and her scent was a little off. While other men drooled over her beauty, I was quick to look the other way.

Still, with her father watching from the buffet table, it would be rude of me to deny her request. "Very well," I said without much enthusiasm.

She didn't seem to mind because she flashed me that flirty little smile of hers as she attached herself to my arm.

Within seconds, we had joined the crowd. As a group, we flowed with the music. I closed my eyes and concentrated on the sound, focusing on the different instruments. When I was younger, I had learned discipline by picking up a violin. Since running my own company, I hadn't found the time to pick it up again.

Suddenly, a shot of electricity stabbed through my chest. I sucked in a lungful of air as my eyes widened.

"Is everything alright?" Sidney asked when she noted my tension.

"Yes," I answered as I resumed our dancing.

It didn't take me long to find her.

My heart surged and my body felt like it was going to lurch forward on its own accord.

She was stunning.

Her neck, long and lean, was highlighted by the straps that wrapped around it. All I had to do was tug at those straps and her lovely chest would be mine for the taking. I narrowed my eyes. Was I imagining her nipples poking through the fabric or was she truly excited?

Vern and I locked eyes. I nodded but there was a stern look on my face. He knew my circumstances and yet he insisted on tormenting me with the woman I could not have.

The song we were dancing to came to an end and I excused myself from Sidney. The crowd parted way as I made my way towards the young couple. "May I have a word?" I said, addressing Vern. "Privately."

Ari glanced my way. "Is there a problem?" She had a hand on her hip. "I didn't know you played for the other team and that you wanted my date so badly. I thought I had to worry about the other girls but I guess I have to worry about you too."

"Are you implying that I like Vern?" I spat.

"It certainly seems that way."

Vern stepped between us. "There's no need to fight. There's plenty of me to go around." He winked at Ari. "I will only be a moment."

"Fine." Ari didn't look very happy but she nonetheless walked away.

I took Vern by the elbow and dragged him towards the balcony. The pair of security guards nodded at our presence and stepped aside.

Outside, the air was considerably cooler. It helped to clear my head. "What lies have you been feeding her?" I turned on Vern, nearly pinning him against the wall. "Why does she think –"

"I doubt she really believes that," Vern interjected. "I mean, you pretty much scream heterosexuality."

I took a step closer, my upper lip curling. "I am not here to play games. You know better than to engage with her. The Aetos have a claim –"

"Fuck the claim." He pushed me aside. "They've had years to take her and yet she's completely unmarked. As far as I'm concerned, she's ours for the taking."

"If she's willing," he added. "And only if she's willing."

"So, you agree that the Aetos have lost their chance –"

"No," I answered. "That is not what I said." I leaned against the railing and looked into the distance. There, my clan resided, safe and sound thanks to the peace treaty between the two different fractions of dragons. If I angered them by taking Ari as my own, there was no telling the repercussions I would face. "It would put our people in jeopardy."

"But don't you feel it?" He turned me around so I was forced to look at him. "That inner tug of our instincts telling you that she's the one."

"Don't tell me about that tug." I hung my head. "I felt it ten years ago when she was a teenager and she thought I was one too. It was a torture to know that I was forbidden to have her. That's why I pushed her away and that's why she resents me now."

Vern frowned. "But do you not think there is a way to remedy that?"

"I do not know," I admitted. "I can see it in her eyes that she does not trust me. It will take a miracle for her to accept our dragon lineage or that she is destined to mate with us."

"So, you're just going to give up?" Vern punched my arm. "I refuse to accept that. Whenever you want something, you always find a way to get it. Ari shouldn't be any different." He squared his shoulders and held his ground. It was the first real time that he had stood against me. "I am not letting her slip away from us."

I sighed. "You're right. As much as I want to avoid fighting with the Aetos, I cannot keep repressing my instincts. I must have her."

A wild grin flashed across his face, "Now that's the Lyle I know and love."

"But first we must be certain that she is strong enough to carry our offspring."

"Have you seen her hips? Those are child-bearing hips if I've ever seen them." He glanced through the glass door, eyes wandering over her body.

I couldn't stop myself from doing the same. She had the body of a goddess and I could see myself worshiping every inch.

"Let me talk to her. Keep Sidney off my tail. She likes to hover around me like a gnat."

"Leave it to me." Vern sauntered through the doors with a certain swagger. He had no trouble finding Sidney and engaging her in conversation.

Meanwhile, I made my way over to Ari who stood by one of the open windows.

I cleared my throat so I wouldn't scare her but she stared all the same. Doing so, she accidentally spilled some champagne onto her chest. She gasped.

Without thinking, I swiped a napkin from a nearby table and wiped her down.

A second later, I felt a slap against my cheek. My skin prickled with pain as I reeled back. The entire hall descended into silence as everyone looked our way.

"What do you think you're doing, you pig?"

"I was trying to help you!" I protested with a growl. "Do you really think I would grope you like that?"

"I wouldn't put it past you."

"Funny for someone who accused me of liking men a few minutes ago."

She groaned. "Ugh, why are you such a pain in my ass?"

"Look, I didn't mean anything by it. I was simply trying to get the champagne off before it stained your nice dress. I don't understand why that's such a crime."

"Because I'm not some blonde –"

"Are you jealous of Sidney?" I scoffed at the idea.

"So, Sidney's her name, is it?"

"Yes. And if you must know, I only danced with her because her father is one of my investors. If he wasn't here, I wouldn't have given her the time of day."

Ari crossed her arms over her chest. "Do you want to tell me why you're here? Clearly, you want something from me."

I held out my hand. "I want to dance."

She parted her lips and for a second, I expected her rejection. I could almost hear it but then she placed her hand in mine.

"This better be one hell of a dance to make up for the fact that you stuck your hands down my dress."

"I never aim to disappoint," I said as I whisked her away. Our very first dance was one with a quick tempo. I held her tightly and practically lifted her off the ground as I stepped in time with my fellow dancers.

When it came time to change partners, I held her even closer so that every inch of her body touched mine. This disrupted the flow of the dance but I hardly cared. Now that I held her in my arms, I couldn't fathom letting her go.

My hand dropped to the lovely fullness of her ass. To my surprise, she didn't push me away like I thought she would. Instead, I felt her press her hips forward, like her body had taken control and it was begging for mine.

The steps quickened but I kept in pace. I twirled her around and bent her back until the top of her head grazed the floor. To keep her steady, my hand found a hold on the top of her thigh. The skin there was silky and smooth. Oh, how I yearned to explore her every secret.

I pulled her back up and our faces nearly crashed together. She did not breathe as she looked into my eyes. Turmoil brewed there, I could sense it. If I had to guess, her past was fighting the current attraction she felt. "Let go," I whispered against her ear before I spun her around and caught her during the very next beat.

Her chest heaved with the marathon I was putting her through, but I wanted to see her sweat. Better yet, I wanted to hear her screaming my name.

My dragon surfaced and for a second, my eyes shifted to their natural form.

Had she noticed?

The song ended.

Ari panted. "Whoa… Okay, you surprised me there. I didn't think you'd be such an amazing dancer." Her hairdo had come partly undone, leaving her with a rather messy look. It was sexy as all hell. That, combined with what she was wearing. All I wanted to do was pounce on her right then and there.

My eyes fell on her cleavage, making things even worse.

"I need a glass of water or something."

"Here, let me get it for you." I left her for a moment and returned with some ice water. She took it with a look of gratefulness before chugging most of it down.

When she was done, I guided her towards a private lounge, closed off from the ballroom.

She raised a brow, eyeing with suspicion. "I don't know if I like being alone with you…" she said but her voice wavered, laced with uncertainty.

"I just wanted to thank you for a good time. I haven't danced like that in quite some time."

"Where did you learn to do that?"

"Rome."

"You're kidding, right?"

"Not at all. I spent a summer there. It was the summer after ¬–"

"Let me guess, you hated me so much that you had to go to a whole other continent just to get away from me," she said. Her stance was a defensive one, but I could tell by the tone of her voice that saying those words pained her. It was then that I realized that in my attempt to protect myself, I had injured her emotionally. By pushing her away, I had broken her heart.

"No." I shook my head as I reached out to grab her hands. She pulled back and rose to her feet. "Ari."

She didn't bother to look at me.

"I never meant to hurt you." I stood behind her. When she did not turn around, I placed my hand on her waist and pulled her towards me. As soon as I did, I saw the glassiness of her eyes and the tears streaking down her cheeks. My heart tightened at the sight because I knew I was the cause of her grief. All this time and she still felt the pain of my actions.

Gently, I wiped away her tears with my thumb. My hand lingered by the side of her face, cupping it against my palm.

"I know it probably doesn't mean much but I really am sorry."

She turned her head and tried to slip away from my grasp but I held her by the arm.

"All I ask is that we start fresh. I am willing to bury the hatch if you are too."

She finally looked me in the eye. "Meaning?"

"You show up to work Monday morning."

Her expression changed to one of surprise as the brows rose on her forehead. "What are you talking about?"

"I have decided to hire you –"

"But I thought you said I wasn't qualified for the job."

I shrugged. "I have a feeling you're a quick learner."

She bit her bottom lip in contemplation.

"Look, I did my research. I know you need the money and that you're in no position to turn me down."

"Fine." She conceded. "You're right. I do need this job whether I want to work with you or not."

"Still not very fond of me, huh?"

"A single dance isn't going to erase our history," she answered as she made her way for the door.

Before she could grab hold of the handle, I stopped her. The hair on the back of my neck stood on edge. My nostrils flared as I caught wind of a foreign scent.

What was that?

Just then, the lights flickered.

Overhead, a lightbulb shattered.

Ari screamed with fright, but I had her in my arms in an instant, holding her in a protective embrace.

It was then that it dawned on me.

That smell... it was... Aetos.

They were here – spying on me.

I held Ari all the tighter. She leaned against my chest, confiding in my strength. And at that moment, I experienced something I had never felt before. It stirred inside the depths of my heart.

Warmth.

Chapter 11 Ari

Monday morning.

I was wearing the same skirt from my interview but with a different blouse. Hopefully, no one would notice.

My feet were killing me as I walked the rest of the way from the bus stop. I tried to adjust my footing but to no avail.

By some miracle, I reached the headquarters at exactly 8:30 A.M. – just as Lyle had asked me to. Truth be told, I still don't know why I agreed to work for a man I hated.

Because, deep down, you want to like him. You want to forgive him. That little voice at the back of my head was starting to become really damn annoying. It didn't know what it was talking about.

Eager to get this over with, I tugged on the front door only to find it closed. "What the hell?" I tugged on it a little harder this time but it was still as locked as ever.

I fished for my phone out of my pocket, ready to give Lyle a call.

That's when a red Ferrari came speeding around the bend. It flew down the street and eased into the building's parking garage. I didn't even wait for it to park as I marched right up to it and stand with arms folded in front of the driver's side.

Lyle got out, dressed in a suit.

"What the hell?" I spat the second he could hear me.

He looked down at me, eyebrow raised. His lips twitched slightly like he was amused by my display of anger.

"You were the one who nearly ran me over!"

"Hmm?"

"The day it was downpouring. The day right before my interview. You were driving like a maniac."

"I was late for a meeting., h3e answered like it was the most obvious thing in the world. "And I couldn't afford to be late."

"You nearly ran me over!" I repeated. "I saw my life flash before my eyes."

"There's no need to be so dramatic."

"I bet you did it on purpose!" I accused.

"Of course not." He rested a hand on my shoulder but I pulled away.

"You didn't even get out of your car to ask if I was okay or not."

"I already told you. I had a meeting to go to and I couldn't afford to be late –"

I slapped him before he could say another word. It was only after I did that, I realized that doing so would probably cost me my job and boy, did I need this paycheck. My heart stopped, waiting for him to lash out at me.

"Okay, I probably deserved that," he said, his voice as calm as water on a warm summer's day. "But..." An edge crept into his voice as he grabbed me by the wrist. "If you know what's good for you, you'll think before you do something."

Was he threatening me?

Fear swept underneath my skin, leaving me cold.

He dropped my wrist and proceeded to the side door. There, he took out an ID card and ran it through the scanner. "And so long as we're working together, you will address me as your superior."

A copper taste rose at the back of my throat. I should have known that his little act at the gala was just a façade to get me to accept his job proposal. He wasn't sorry at all. He was still the same ol' asshole.

Down the hall, we waited for the elevator. It arrived within seconds of pushing the button.

I hesitated. "Maybe I should take the stairs," I said despite the fact that my feet were covered in blisters. Any unnecessary walking would be torturous. Yet, it seemed better than being trapped in a small space with a madman.

"Get in," was all he said. His eyes darkened as his tone was one of pure authority.

I couldn't have defied him even if I wanted to.

The doors closed shut behind me, nearly pinching the fabric of my skirt between them. Lyle was quick to pull me out of harm's way. "Careful," he hissed.

It was strange. In a way, it seemed like he was trying to protect me but why did he have to be such a dick about it?

"I don't get you," I mumbled underneath my breath. I didn't even realize I had spoken my thoughts aloud until I felt the weight of his stare.

"Let's get one thing straight here, shall we? This here is a business. The way we act and the way we handle things will decide whether his business is successful or not. So, if you'd like a paycheck every week then I would suggest you take this seriously."

Ding!

As soon as the doors opened, he walked out. There was confidence in his every step. More than that, Lyle walked with a certain swagger that only came when you knew you owned the place.

As much as I hated to admit it, his alpha attitude was sexy as hell. He was the kind of man who wouldn't take no for an answer. He knew exactly what he wanted.

I only wished he wanted me.

With a sigh, I followed him.

This was going to be a nightmare of a job. I could already tell that Lyle was going to drive me insane.

But what choice did I have? It was either take his offer or get thrown to the streets for failing to pay rent. In this case, Lyle was definitely the lesser of two evils.

And the more attractive one, that's for sure.

Besides, I only needed to put up with him long enough for me to find another job worth keeping.

Chapter 12 Vern

That evening.

"So, how was it?" I asked as soon as Lyle walked through the door.

He did not answer me.

I turned around and saw him slump into the kitchen table.

"Rough day at work?"

Silence.

Knowing it was pointless to try and have a conversation, I went back to cooking. The smell of sautéed onions wafted into the air. I added a bit of condensed cream to the mix and waited for it to bubble overtop the pasta, coating it to utter perfection.

I was practically drooling by the time I brought two heaping plates over to the table. I didn't bother to wait for Lyle to dig in. If he wanted to starve himself then that was his decision.

"Do you know how difficult it is to know that she resents me?"

I looked up as I slurped a particularly long noodle. "Who?"

"Who else?" He huffed as he finally picked up his fork and stabbed it into his meal.

"Jeez. I can assure you that the noodles are already dead."

Lyle shot me such a dirty glare that I immediately ceased my teasing. This was why he was alpha. He just had this aura about him. To go against him was blasphemous.

"Alright, so Ari gave you a hard time today?"

"No. She did exactly as I said but I could see it in her eyes. She doesn't like working for me." He kept twirling the pasta around his fork, gathering it up, but never actually eating it.

"Were you harsh with her?"

"Harsh? No, I don't think so. I believe I acted as any good boss should," he said.

I grabbed my glass of water and swirled it around. Sometimes, Lyle didn't take criticism very well and I had a feeling that this would be one of those times. "Well, you see, sometimes you come across the wrong way to those who don't know you very well."

He pressed his lips together, eyes burning into me.

"So, you might think you were acting as you should and Ari, on the other hand, might think you're a massive dick."

I could almost hear his teeth grinding together. His nostrils flared. A vein in his temple started to throb.

Uh-oh.

I had really pissed him off now. I prepared myself to duck for cover but instead, he took a deep breath and the tension from his body seemed to disappear. "I suppose I do not realize it. I am so accustomed to keeping people at arm's length that I might come across as being rather cold."

"Yes, you could say that," I agreed with some trepidation. "And if you want Ari as our mate, you'll need to be nicer to her."

We finished the rest of our meal in silence.

To my surprise, Lyle picked up the dishes and rinsed them off before placing them in the dishwasher. As he wiped his hands on a rag, he turned to look at me. "What happens if she refuses us? There have been plenty of humans to renounce the existence of dragons. She may never want to see us again."

"You're nervous, aren't you?" I asked. It was rare to see Lyle looking this vulnerable.

"Do you blame me? Deep down, I know she's the one we have been waiting for. Everything is telling me that I need to be with her and yet..."

"And yet...?" I repeated, urging him to continue.

"This feels like a mistake."

"How so?"

"At the gala, I felt their presence."

"You mean the Aetos?"

He nodded, "they were there. I am sure of it. No doubt they sent spies to watch us. They must know about our interest."

I stepped forward. "Well, if they want her so bad, they'll have to get through us first."

"That is what worries me. Our numbers are dwindling. The last thing we need is another war on our hands and that's exactly what I'm instigating ¬–"

"You are only following your natural born right as alpha to take the girl you choose to be your mate. If they want to challenge that, then so be it."

He shook his head. "You do not understand. The weight of the clan falls on my shoulders. I am the strongest alpha and therefore, everyone looks at me for guidance. If I lead our clan to war, what will they think?"

"Perhaps it is high time we return and have a word with one of the elders," I said. "It has been a while."

Lyle shook his head. "I have been avoiding it, but I suppose I ignore it any longer."

Together, we headed for the back door. The porch needed a good washing but that was a task for another day.

Lyle was the first to transform. It happened in the blink of an eye. One second, he was a man and in another, he was a dragon. Even after witnessing his dragon form countless times, it still impressed me. His scales were of the darkest hue that at times they looked purple. Each one folded over the other in a perfect crisscross pattern.

He craned his long neck and looked at me. His eyeball alone was almost as big as I was.

Coming? His voice echoed inside my head with a serpentine sort of hiss.

I nodded and braced myself for the pain to come. Being a beta meant that I could never fully transform. Instead, my wings protruded from my back, ripping through my flesh. I cried out as my head throbbed with the agony of sporting brand new appendages.

Finally, they stretched and settled into place.

I was able to breathe again.

Lyle did not wait another second. He took off like a bullet through the sky. His body decimated the clouds. The moisture rolled off his body and saturated the ground.

I followed as best I could. It was much harder considering the fact that I was a hundred times smaller. Nevertheless, we reached the clan at nearly the same moment.

He landed in a giant clearing made especially for dragons. I touched down beside him, careful to avoid being squashed by one of his giant talons.

I wiped the sweat from my brow and attempted to catch my breath as he returned to his human state. Lyle hadn't even broken a sweat. Sometimes, I truly envied that man.

As we walked through the clan, people bowed their heads in Lyle's direction. He acknowledged their respect, but it was clear by the way he cut through the land that he was focused only on his destination.

We reached a long, wooden building. A pink-colored smoke arose from the chimney. The elders were in the middle of prayer. Lyle did not seem to care as he barged right in.

The elders immediately halted their chanting and looked up at the dragon. "It has come to my attention that the Aetos have reverted to spying. They follow me."

"We know," answered the oldest clan's member. "We have foreseen what is to come." His voice was gravelly and full of wisdom. All those who heard him were forced to listen. "You have encountered the girl. I once told you to stay away from this girl – that she would bring you nothing but trouble. It is true." The others nodded in agreement. "But as a true alpha, you could not help yourself. She is yours and you are hers. To ignore that feeling would mean going against your own instincts."

The elder rose to his feet and leaned heavily on a wooden staff. He stepped forward until he was standing beside the alpha.

"We know that you will claim her as your own and that this will incite a war between the two clans. We are prepared for it and we will stand by your side as you make your decision." The elder rubbed his thumb across Lyle's right cheek, smearing it with red paint. "You have our blessing. Now, do what your heart tells you to do. The rest will follow."

He then turned to my direction and smeared the red dye on my left cheek.

"You know your place beside the alpha. Protect him from himself."

With that, we excused ourselves.

I was thankful for the fresh air. I had never liked the incense they burned during prayer.

"What do you think?" I asked as soon as we reentered the clearing.

"I think it is time for us to get us a girl," he grinned. There was a burning in his eyes that spoke of excitement. "But we take things slow and we do things right. I do not want to scare her."

I nodded. "I will follow your lead, whatever it might be."

Chapter 13 Ari

A few days later.

For some reason, Lyle was much more pleasant to work with but he was far from being a ray of sunshine. He still snapped from time to time. Maybe the stress of running such a big company was weighing down on his patience.

I thought about this as I ran the copy machine. Of course, the paper jammed. I opened it up and groaned. By the looks of it, I had a real problem on my hands. I tried to pull out the crumpled-up pieces of paper but all I managed to do was break a nail.

It was one of those nasty breaks that tear right through the nail bed. I cursed under my breath and tried to shake away the pain that throbbed through the tip of my finger. When I dared to look at the damage, I found I was bleeding. "Goddamn it." I was about to find myself a bandage when Lyle appeared at the doorway. I bumped right into that solidly built chest of his. It was like crashing into a wall.

He caught me before I could trip. The strength of his arms bulged through his every muscle as I rested my hand on his forearm. "Are you okay?" He asked as he motioned to my injured finger. He took my hand with the utmost gentleness. It was strange for such a hulking individual to have a feather-like touch. "Let's get this taken care of. I wouldn't want to get blood all over the place."

I followed him back to his office where he closed – and locked – the door behind him.

Goosebumps traveled along the length of my arm when I realized I was alone with this man.

Suddenly, he picked me up by the hips and set me down on his desk.

"You know, there are... chairs," I said nervously.

"Yes," he responded as he looked through his drawers. "But this makes it easier for me." A second later, he was between my legs. "Give me your hand."

I did as he asked.

He peeled away the backing from the bandage and wrapped it around my finger. "You should be more careful next time. I wouldn't want you hurting yourself." His voice was soft and tender. His eyes were kinder, too, like he was looking at me in a brand-new light.

"I don't understand," I whispered aloud. "What changed?"

"Hmm?"

"You've changed."

"Have I?"

His closeness was throwing me off my guard. The hairs on the back of my neck stood on edge as our gazes crossed. I found myself getting lost in the depths of his eyes.

Our faces gravitated toward one another like a couple of magnets. I held my breath.

His warm breath brushed against my lips and it sent a spark of excitement straight into my heart. It skipped a beat before charging into an impossible tempo that left me light headed.

What was going on right now?

There was a knock on the door and our moment of magic was shattered by the sound. My cheeks burned with the realization that I had nearly kissed my boss – the man I was supposed to hate. Quickly, I dropped down from his desk.

"Thanks," I said before I left.

Back in the copy room, my whole body felt like it was up in flames. I couldn't get Lyle's face out of my head.

"What's wrong with me?" I whispered as I ran my fingers through my hair. "I shouldn't be feeling this way."

Just then, one of the interns walked in.

She was the sort of girl that looked all put together. Her clothes hugged every inch of her body like they had been custom made just for her. On the other hand, I looked like a soup sandwich in my baggy blouse and too long dress pants.

"Hey!" She said with a flick of her bangs. "You must be Lyle's personal assistant."

"Um... yes, I am." I didn't think to ask how she knew.

"I applied to that position myself," she continued. "But I guess you were just better qualified." She sighed. "I bet it must be a dream come true working for such a handsome billionaire." There was a dreamy look in her eyes. "What's it like?"

She turned on me so suddenly that I didn't know what to say.

"Oh, come on, don't hold out on me." She stepped forward, practically cornering me against the wall. "What's he like? Does he ever hit on you?"

"Um... I hardly think it's appropriate for us to talk about such things," I said. This felt like a trap from the HR department and I wasn't about to fall for it. "And for the record, Lyle is a professional. He does not flirt with his employees. So, quit dreaming."

The woman frowned and a moment later, she was gone.

I felt like I could breathe again. What was that all about? Was she really fawning over Lyle or was there something malicious in her actions?

It wasn't unlikely that she found him attractive because he was, well, sexy as hell. The thought filled me with a fit of jealousy that threatened to make me sick. What did it matter anyway? It's not like I stood a chance with the guy. Besides, he wanted nothing to do with me – that much he had made clear a long, long time ago. I just wasn't his type and I wasn't about to change my ways to please someone so arrogantly selfish.

With this thought in mind, I went back to fixing the copy machine. It took some elbow grease but I finally managed to get it working again.

Then came the boredom of waiting for all the pages to print. Time crawled by at a molasses pace. I yawned and leaned against the wall.

When I closed my eyes, there he was. His chiseled face haunted me followed by the coolness of his eyes. Did he want me or was he just playing a cruel game?

I tried to steel my heart, but I couldn't keep lying to myself. I liked Lyle – more than I wanted to admit.

***

Finally, the day came to an end and I clocked out of the system. Although I was no longer getting paid, I checked my inbox one more time and started to respond to a few straggling emails.

Most of them consisted of setting up meetings for Lyle. Just looking at his schedule made me feel tired. Most of his days were booked solid.

I stared at the screen as if that would help make some space.

"Still working?"

When I looked up, there he was. He had ditched his coat, leaving him in a light blue dress shirt that complimented his olive-toned skin. His sleeves were rolled, revealing the bulk of his forearms. Even as he relaxed against the doorframe, I could see his muscles rippling underneath the skin.

I gulped, trying to keep a hold of myself. "Just responding to a couple of emails," I said, wetting my lips. "I'll be done in just a minute."

He stepped into my office and grabbed an apple I had taken from the breakroom. He bit into it. The juices ran down his chin and nearly fell onto his shirt before he wiped it away with the back of his hand. There was just something so carnal about the way he did so that had me burning up.

All I could imagine was his tongue between my folds. I wanted to feel him lapping at my juices, eager for every last drop.

I held my breath as he rounded my desk and leaned over. It almost looked like he was about to run his hand underneath my skirt but instead, he simply threw away the half-eaten apple in the trash.

"If you'd like, I can give you a ride home?"

"After you nearly ran me over? Not going to happen." I closed my laptop and pushed past him so I could grab my jacket. He beat me to it and held it at arm's length so I couldn't reach. "And especially not now when you're being a jerk."

He grinned and lowered it. I was about to snatch it away from him but he pulled away at the last moment. "You're so quick to anger," he whispered. "But I kind of like it." His voice was low and sensuous.

As I tried to come up with a response, he eased the sleeves over my arms, just as Vern had on the night of the gala.

Guilt stabbed into my chest. That's right – Vern.

I had been so caught up with my new job and my new boss that he completely slipped my mind. Clearly, he was the better of the two and yet, I couldn't keep my eyes off the billionaire. He was like that forbidden fruit I could not have. That only made me want him all the more.

"Thanks," I mumbled underneath my breath. "But I'm not going to forgive you."

"You aren't going to let that go, are you?"

"Nope." I walked out of my office. Lyle was hot on my tail. As I locked the door, he hovered right behind me. When I turned around, he pushed me against the wall. I gasped, eyes going wide. I looked around but the hallway was empty.

"I'm not a man who takes no for an answer," he said.

I pushed him away by placing both hands on his chest. It was obvious he had allowed me to move him because if he had wanted to resist me, I would have been powerless to stop him. "And I'm not the type of girl that falls for a guy like you." I tried to keep my voice steady.

"As far as I'm concerned, you're just my boss and nothing is ever going to change that." I held my head up high and turned on my heels.

It was difficult to say those things when the lustful side of me wanted nothing more than to fall into bed with that man. Could you blame me when he was so damn sexy? I mean, it's not every day that you meet a Greek God.

These thoughts burned at my cheeks and I had to push them away. Already, the fantasies were starting to fester and as a result, wetness gathered between my legs. It got worse as my mind undressed him. First went his shirt, revealing a chiseled midsection. Then his pants. And of course,...

Ding!

The elevator arrived. I quickened inside. The doors were about to close when someone stuck their hand between them.

Lyle.

He invaded the space, his thick presence making it hard to breathe. My heart thumped against my chest, threatening to explode.

Then, he positioned himself a little closer and I could feel the heat radiating from his body. He was like a human furnace. I wanted to melt against him and ease into his embrace, but I couldn't. He would only hurt me as he did all those years ago.

Thankfully, the elevator reached the bottom and we both went our separate ways. I held onto my purse tightly as I walked down the street towards the bus stop. Overhead, the sky was dark with clouds. I prayed the rain would hold off for the next few minutes.

I waited for the crosswalk. A chill rolled down my spine, making me shiver. I glanced over my shoulder. For some reason, it felt like someone was watching me but as far as I could tell, I was the only person there.

The light failed to change so I looked both ways and crossed to the other side. My instincts were telling me to run. Something wasn't right. I kept looking over my shoulder but there was no one to be seen.

"It's fine..." I told myself but I wasn't convinced.

My heart was pounding by the time I caught the bus. The driver nodded and offered a smile.

I settled into the back and looked out the window. I couldn't be sure but it looked like something – or someone – was lurking in the shadows of where I had stood only moments before. I swallowed back the lump of fear.

It's all in your head. I tried to tell myself. Or, is it?

Chapter 14 Lyle

Something told me to follow her so that's what I did. I waited until she had a bit of a lead before I trailed at the distance.

She kept looking over her shoulder but she wasn't glancing in my direction. Instead, she kept checking the other side of the street. Oddly enough, all the street lamps were off, casting everything in a deep, dark shadow. This was not a coincidence. Someone had tampered with those lights and I had a good hunch on who that someone was.

I waited until I was sure Ari wouldn't look back. Only then did I hasten into the darkness. I plucked a thin individual by the collar and slammed him into the brick wall. "What do you think you're doing?" I snarled.

The man grinned, exposing a row of sharp teeth.

I ducked just in time to avoid a crushing blow to the head. A second later, I was struck in the gut by someone's knee. I was able to hold my stand and pivot the momentum into my attacker. With my hand around his neck, I threw him to the ground.

The thin individual looked thunderstruck like I had just turned water into wine.

"You're making a mistake," growled the one I currently had pinned underneath my body. "She is ours."

"And yet, you did not make your mark in all these years. What are you waiting for?"

My rival grinned. "You."

It was then that I noticed movement further down the street. Ari was no longer in my sights. My blood ran cold when I realized that these two members of the Aetos were just a distraction.

I left them in the dust, their laughs penetrating through my skull.

How had I allowed myself to become such a fool?

I jogged towards the bend. To my relief, Ari was nearing the bus stop. I watched her as she fidgeted from one foot to the other. She craned her neck, hoping to spot the oncoming bus but the road was deserted.

"She's a pretty one, isn't she?" Came a deep, gravel-filled voice.

"Hector." I straightened to my full height and rolled back my shoulders. "I should have known you were behind all this."

"And yet, you choose to get involved." His serpentine tongue flicked from his mouth and passed along his lips. "You Ragnis always want what you cannot have." He stepped forward. His dress shoes were gilded with gold and I did not fail to notice that they had been sharped to a deadly point. A man like Hector would not hesitate to use them as a weapon.

"At least we have the decency to let women mate us out of their own free will. We do not kidnap them into our clan as you do." Venom dripped from my every word. Oh, how my fists burned to throw a punch at this man's face. That dirty grin of his needed to be wiped off the face of the planet.

"I bet it burns you up inside to know that she'll be mine."

"Over my dead body."

"That can be arranged." He leaned against a nearby lamppost, acting as if this were a casual conversation. "I'd like to see you try."

"You know, I would take you up on your offer but without that little beta of yours by your side, I doubt we could call it a fair fight."

I scoffed. "We both know the Ragnis are stronger. We have been for centuries."

"But your numbers are dwindling." He strolled forward. "Your method of finding mates is awfully inefficient and you're paying the price for it."

I could not stand his voice any longer. I lunged forward but he sidestepped my attack. That was the thing about the Aetos – they were fast.

In the blink of an eye, Hector stood behind me. He snapped his walking cane behind my back. Pain radiated down my spine as I fell to my knees. "I think this little crush of yours has made you weak, Lyle."

I whipped around and aimed for his legs, hoping to get him off balance.

"This really is pathetic." He kicked me in the thigh and I felt the jolt of pain as his shoe tore through my flesh. "How are you supposed to protect the woman you love when you cannot even protect yourself?" He circled around me like a predator preparing to pounce on his flesh.

I waited, calculating when to make my next move. If I wanted to win this, I needed to stick to logic.

He snapped his fingers and his beta, a blonde by the name of Percy, emerged from the shadows. He stood right behind Ari. "Now, all I need to do is give the word and you'll never see her again."

I forced myself to take a deep breath. "But you don't actually want her, do you?"

"Hmm, I might consider having some fun with her. She looks a little inexperienced but I am sure I can teach her exactly what I like." He was only saying these things to piss me off and frankly, it was working. "But you're right. She's not my prime objective." With that, he snapped his fingers once more and the beta disappeared.

I looked up and Hector, too, had vanished.

My skin prickled with suspicion. Clearly, my rivals were up to something and I didn't like it one bit.

Quickly, I turned my attention to Ari. She was still standing by the bus stop, safe and sound.

I was about to call out to her but, at that moment, the bus arrived. She hastened inside and sat in the back. I could almost feel her fear like we were connected on an emotional level.

The bus took off. I wasn't convinced that they would leave her alone, so I did a quick transformation and took to the sky. Once I was high enough, I shifted to my true form and followed the vehicle as it followed its route through the town.

My wings flapped with such raw power that it ruffled the leaves of the trees below me.

If someone happened to spot me, it could cause quite a bit of trouble and I already had enough to deal with. But right now, I didn't particularly care whether or not I kept the secret of dragons sheltered from the public. All that mattered was assuring Ari's well-being.

The bus was nearing her house and I tried to convince myself that maybe they had decided to back off.

Wishful thinking, came that voice in the back of my head.

I scanned the area, looking for any sign of a threat but the thing about the Aetos is that they are ridiculously hard to track. Those that are well-trained almost become invisible against the wind.

My nose was dutifully searching the air for any foreign scent but as far as I could tell, none of my enemies had stuck around.

I relaxed ever so slightly.

Big mistake.

Abruptly, something slammed into me. It felt like a cannonball. A few of my ribs cracked underneath the impact.

I fell, losing altitude before I remembered to beat my wings.

Then came another attack. This time, I was able to turn my head and clamp my jaw around their neck. The dragon screeched as I threw him into the forest. Trees fell and toppled over his carcass.

By a hair's breadth, I managed to avoid an incoming attack. He aimed for my flank, so I retaliated with a good ol' kick. My assailant went flying, his own blood following after him.

I ducked down before rising into the clouds. And that's when I came face to face with Hector. Oh, if he wanted a battle, he was going to get one.

We charged into one another, our bodies colliding with a horrible clap of sound. Anyone who heard it would think it was a crack of thunder.

I checked on the progress of Ari's bus. My distraction opened up a window of opportunity. Hector took his chance and tackled me straight to the ground. My body created a crater in the soft Earth. I groaned and attempted to fight him off but as I did so, the rest of the clan circled around us.

They were syncing up for an ambush.

This was not looking good.

Chapter 15 Ari

I got off the bus stop and headed toward my home. Again, I felt like someone was watching me. Yet, there was no one around. I paused and tilted my head to the side, hoping to hear something.

Silence.

It was an eerie sort of silence that had the hairs on my arm standing on edge.

I swallowed back my fears and continued forward. After a few steps, I rummaged through my bag and pulled out my keys. I held them between my fingers like I intended to use them as brass knuckles. Having them at my disposal calmed me a bit and I was able to return to a relatively normal pace.

Click. Click. Click.

My heels echoed against the silence. It was almost like I wasn't meant to be there.

Crash!

I jumped out of my skin, my heart skipping a beat.

Overhead, the clouds darkened. Strange shadows passed through them. I had never seen anything like it before. Must be one heck of a storm on the horizon. I was about to take a step forward when another thunderclap boomed through the land. It was so loud, I feared I had become partially deaf.

Then, something fell out of the sky. It looked like some sort of meteor rocketing towards the tree line.

The ground shook underneath my feet when it made a crash landing.

"What the fuck?" Was all I could say before I started running. For some strange reason, I was running straight towards it. I tried to tell my body to turn around but it would not listen to me. There was some sort of invisible force dragging me towards the scene. I couldn't resist it.

Even as I tripped over logs and foliage, I continued forward. I was desperate to see what had fallen from the sky.

Thorns snagged against my clothes, tearing them to shreds. Well, there goes one of the only outfits I could use to work.

The thought vanished from my head when I walked into a wall of darkness. Suddenly, it was hard to breathe. It felt like a two-ton elephant had settled onto my shoulders.

My mind screamed for me to get away – to leave this evil place – and yet my heart urged me forward.

I had managed to retrieve my phone from my pocket. The flashlight did little to illuminate my path. Still, it was better than stumbling around in the dark. I held onto nearby tree trunks for support as the forest grew thicker and thicker.

Was I even going in the right direction?

I turned ever so slowly and saw that everything looked exactly the same. I blinked as if that would highlight the path I had taken. Great. I was lost. This was exactly what I needed.

Unsure of where to go next, I hesitated. What would happen if I failed to find my way out? It was well-known that wolves hunted on this land. To a pack of carnivores, I probably looked like a pretty good snack.

Then, I heard something. It was a whimper of sorts that had my heart in a state of agony. I clutched at my heart, my knees knocking together with a lack of strength.

There it was again, louder this time.

What was that?

There was only one way to find out.

Clearly, I had lost my mind. What I was doing was completely insane and yet, I couldn't even think of turning back. It was as if some sort of primal instinct had come alive inside of me. Something was hurt and I needed to find out what.

Up ahead, I came across a river. It was pretty wide and the current was strong. I didn't know if it was shallow enough for me to cross and frankly, I didn't want to risk it. I turned to my left, looking for some way to cross when I encountered a fallen tree, laid along the width of the river.

Perfect.

All I needed to do was keep my balance but considering how much of a klutz I was, that was easier said than done. Still, I clambered on top of it and held out my arms like a trapeze artist.

Why are you doing this? Came that voice in my head. This is crazy.

"I know," I spoke aloud. "But I can't explain it. I have to do this."

A flash of red caught my attention. For a second there, it looked like a plume of fire.

It happened again. The explosion of light much bigger this time around. Through it, I caught a glimpse of two oversized creatures.

What were those things?

Instead of being afraid, I was intrigued, especially by the larger of the two. It turned its head in my direction.

Crash!

I flinched as it took a hit. Doing so, I lost my footing. I would have fallen into the water but at that exact moment, something snatched me up. I kept my eyes closed as we soared higher and higher. If there was one thing I didn't like, it was heights.

"Ari."

My heart stuttered at the sound of that familiar voice.

"Vern?" I spat in disbelief.

"None other." He grinned.

"Wait! You have wings!" I exclaimed. "Dragon wings."

"You catch on pretty quick. Most people guess I'm part bat and then speculate I'm a vampire or something but that's just ridiculous. They've been extinct for over a hundred years."

I had no idea what he was talking about but it didn't matter because there was a full-fledged dragon coming our way. "Look out!" I screamed, pointing at our threat.

He tightened his hold around my body as he dashed forward, weaving through the sea of trees. I felt the lick of a couple of branches but I was sure that Vern was taking the brunt of it.

The dragon opened its maw, revealing a neat row of dagger-like teeth. He leaned forward, snapping at Vern.

He jerked suddenly as our assailant ripped through the leathery fold of his wings.

I could see the pain on his face. Despite the fact that I hadn't sustained any injuries, I felt that pain too. It ached like a dull sword through my heart.

"Hold on!" He shouted as he curled his body onto mine. We headed straight for the ground.

I could hear myself screaming.

Crash!

I was ejected out of his grasp and into a large oak tree. My body vibrated like a sounding rod. The bones in my neck felt like they had been shattered into a million pieces. I gasped and fell forward, gasping for air that never came. The edge of my vision started to blur. I tried to blink away the brightness but it persisted.

And then, it took over completely and my body went slack with unconsciousness.

Chapter 16 Vern

Ari looked particularly vulnerable lying in one of the clan's sleeping mats. There was little color in her face and she was burning up. With a frown, I took a washcloth and dipped it into a little bucket of cold water. I rinsed out the access before folding it up and placing it on her forehead. Hopefully, that would help with the fever.

When she failed to stir, I mashed up a salve of berries and medicinal herbs. I knew from experience that they had a rather bitter taste. The berries would help make it taste a little better.

Using my middle finger, I applied it to her lips, dying them a dark shade of crimson. It reminded me of the lipstick she wore during the gala. She had looked so kissable that night. It was a miracle I had kept myself from jumping all over her.

Quickly, I pushed these thoughts from my mind. It was hardly the time.

"Wake up soon," I whispered as I brushed back a strand of her hair. I ran my fingertips along her cheeks and frowned. Perhaps she would be better off living a normal life but it was too late for that now. If we didn't claim her as our own, the Aetos would take her.

Just thinking about it sent the taste of bile into my mouth. I tightened my hand into a fist. I did it with such firmness that my nails scored deep red lines into the skin of my palm.

Her condition was my fault. I should have done a better job of protecting her. Instead, I had lost my hold of her and when I was finally able to find her again, she had already been poisoned by Aetos venom.

It was still up in the air whether she would survive or not.

I got up and released some pent-up energy by walking around the small hut. I paused by the window and watched the pink smoke rise from the prayer circle. What good did praying do? She had been unconscious for three days now.

"Ari…" I spoke her name but my voice was weak. I hadn't left her side in three days and as a result, I had eaten little, not that I had much of an appetite.

I returned to her bed and took her hand in mine. She was so cold. So, I gathered up a few more blankets and layered them on top of her.

As I tucked her in, Lyle walked in.

He was heavily bandaged but he held himself with the same sort of poise he usually posed – confident, cool, and collected. Even after fending off the Aetos assault team, he looked like he was ready to rule the world. Seeing him made me thankful that we were partners. I would hate to have him as an enemy.

"How is she?"

"She isn't fairing any better. I fear the poison was already too involved in her system when we finally got around to treating her."

Lyle placed a hand on my shoulder. "Do not lose faith. I did not fight tooth and nail just to watch her go."

He sat down. The discomfort was plain on his face but he didn't make a single sound of protest.

"How can you be so sure? Aetos poison is some of the strongest in the world. I'm surprised that she has lasted this long."

Lyle turned and looked me straight in the eye. "You have told me that you feel that she is our one true mate, correct?"

I nodded.

"Then it is no wonder that she is as strong as she is. She will one day carry our children. This is but a trial and I know she will get through it."

"You're sounding like one of the elders," I said before sitting down on the edge of the bed. "I suppose I am just worried."

"As am I."

"What are we to do if she never wakes up?"

Lyle shook his head. "Do not think that way. She will wake up, I am sure of it." He ran his finger along the exposed part of her neck. "She still breathes. Blood still runs through her veins and therefore, she will survive."

"If we were to mark her –"

"No." Lyle was quick to reject my idea. "She has not consented to mate with us. We will not take her while she is unconscious."

"But it will give her the strength she needs." I protested.

"If we mate with her then it will be a result of her own free will." His voice was unrelenting and I knew there was no point in trying to argue with the man.

"So, you're suggesting what? That we wait for her to awaken of her own accord?"

"That is exactly what I am suggesting."

I wanted to scream. Any more waiting and I was sure to lose my mind.

"How are you feeling, by the way?" Lyle asked. "Has your wing healed?"

"It's fine," I mumbled. "My injuries were nothing compared to yours."

"But an alpha heals at a much faster rate than a beta. I will be back to normal by the end of the week."

"I still do not believe that you fended off their attack. You were outnumbered six to one."

"You helped."

"Barely."

"Still, I wouldn't be here without your aid. This is why dragons work in pairs. It's more likely that we survive that way."

I bit my lip. There was so much I wanted to say but then I felt Ari starting to stir.

Could it be that she was finally waking up?

Chapter 17 Ari

The darkness was so thick, it felt like I was swimming through a sea of sludge. I tried to wade my way through it but I wasn't going anywhere. It consumed me, covering every inch of my body.

Where was I supposed to go? What was I supposed to do?

In my hopelessness, I prayed for both Lyle and Vern. I wanted them by my side because they were the only people who could truly make me feel safe.

Then, I saw Vern with his big, beautiful dragon wings. Surely, that had been nothing but a figment of my imagination. Vern couldn't possibly be a dragon. Dragons did not exist.

And yet, that strange creature in the distance, it seemed oddly familiar. I recalled some of my fondest memories as a child, curled up by the fire, reading about heroes riding on the backs of giant lizards. Oh, what glory if they were actually real.

I concentrated on this thought and it propelled me forward. The darkness became thinner and thinner until I was finally able to make my way towards a warm, inviting light.

It wrapped me in its comfort and eased me out of the darkness.

That's when I heard their voices. I couldn't quite make out what they were saying but their presence was enough to soothe my nerves.

My body melted into something soft and I became aware of something resting on my forehead. I wanted to remove it but my arms would not budge. They seemed pinned underneath some enormous weight.

"I love her."

It was Lyle.

"I've loved Ari since the first day I saw her but back then I could not have her. I was not strong enough to defend my claim. Now, things have changed. If they want her, they'll have to pry her away from my cold dead body."

"She really is the one, isn't she?" Vern whispered.

"She is."

It was then that the pressure lifted from my head and I was able to open my eyes. The light blinded me. It felt like I was staring into the sun. I whimpered as a throbbing headache pounded through my temples.

"Easy." Vern was by my side in an instant. His body was enough to block out that pesky light.

I dared to open my eyes.

Our faces were incredibly close. His eyes wavered with concern. "Ari..." He whispered, his voice full of relief. "Oh, thank the Heavens you're awake."

Suddenly, he wrapped his arms around me.

I grasped. He was definitely crushing my ribs.

Lyle pulled him away.

"She's still injured. Do not hurt her."

My eyes widened the second I saw the damage done to his body. "What happened?"

"I got in a little... tussle." I could tell that he was lying to make me feel better.

"A little tussle?" I tried to sit up with Vern's help, barely managed to incline my body. "You look like you've been through one of the world wars." I reached for his hand. It was calloused and full of cuts.

He squeezed my fingers ever so gently. "I'm just glad you're okay."

I looked at the two men. "What happened? And I don't want some bullshit answer. I want the truth. All of it."

They exchanged a glance.

"I mean it. If I even get a hint of bullshit, I'll pummel you both to the ground."

Lyle laughed, "Hell! Hath no wrath like a woman scorned."

"That's right."

"Where to start?" Vern spoke aloud. "There's so much we need to tell her."

"The beginning," I suggested. "First of all, I want to know where I am."

"Technically, wouldn't that be the end of our story?"

Lyle held up his hand and we both fell into silence. "We're dragons."

His words slammed into me like a battering ram. So that crazy dream wasn't a dream after all. These men were living, breathing dragons. "I thought dragons were just myths..."

"All myths stem from reality. Humans have a way of avoiding the truth, so they weave stories to make them feel better about the things they refuse to face." As he spoke, he held out his arms.

Two giant wings sprouted from his shoulder blades. They stretched, reaching either side of the hut and still they weren't to their true wingspan. They glittered like they were covered with a coating of black diamonds.

I held my breath as they folded behind his back. They made him look even taller than he was.

"Now, my question to you is whether you will accept us for who we are or if you will forsake us like some of the other humans."

My head was spinning.

This was real.

"Are you a dragon too?" I asked, looking at Vern.

"Yes."

"Can I see –"

He interrupted me with a nod of his head. Unlike Lyle, his face twisted with pain. I wanted to tell him to stop but I was mesmerized by the transformation. His wings were much smaller but they were impressive all the same.

"May I touch them?" I asked.

He turned so his wings were within reach. A few scars lined the leathery skin. I ran my fingers along them, causing him to shiver.

"I'm sorry, did I do something wrong?" I recoiled my hand and studied his face for answers.

"The wings of a dragon are very sensitive and to have them touched by a –"

Lyle jabbed his elbow into Vern's side, silencing him.

"By what?" I demanded.

"You should get some rest," Lyle said, trying to get me to drop the subject but that wasn't going to happen.

"Tell me."

He sighed. "It is complicated."

"This whole thing is complicated. You just told me that you're both dragons. Then you sprouted wings. I'm sure there's nothing that can make this much weirder."

"We should tell her," Vern spoke up. "She has a right to know."

"Very well." Lyle sat down and rested his hands on his knees. "Dragons are a bit peculiar in the way they mate."

"Mate? You mean like?"

"Discovery Channel," Vern said for clarification.

"Um... okay then." Blush crept up my face and settled into my cheeks when I thought about the implications. My thoughts were running at a mile a minute.

"Anyway, as I was saying, dragons are a bit peculiar in the way they mate. Every alpha has a beta." Vern complimented his words by pointing at Lyle and then himself. "In order for a child to be conceived, both must be present."

"So, like..."

Vern nodded, "A threesome."

"This ensures that the child is more likely to survive since it has three parents protecting it," Lyle spoke as if this were all perfectly normal but I was having a hard time keeping up. "But, in addition, the woman must be willing. If she is, a mark will appear on her body, binding her to the dragons who mated her. This became a problem when humans depicted dragons as monsters. Women no longer wanted to mate us. So, some clans decided they would take other measures. They started kidnapping women and giving them drugs so they'd be more... willing."

My eyes widened. "But that's –"

They both nodded. "Disgusting."

Silence settled around us. For a moment, I feared they had done something to me while I slept. I checked my arms for any strange markings.

"We would never do such a thing," Lyle said. "We respect our women and never engage them without their consent. Sometimes, it drives us to madness but it is the price we pay for our chivalry."

"Driven to madness?" I asked.

"All dragons have one true mate. If they are denied that mate, they lose their minds."

"I see..." I fiddled with my fingers and pulled at a loose thread emerging from the blanket I held. "And you two... have you found your one true mate?"

"We have," Vern said as he stared right at me. "You."

"Me?"

"Yes," Lyle said with a nod.

"How long have you known?"

"Since I first laid eyes on you."

"You mean, when we worked together, you already knew?"

"Yes."

"So why did you treat me like such a nuisance? Why did you act like such an asshole? I thought you hated me!"

He laughed. "I did not hate you. I could never imagine hating you."

"Then why?"

He took both my hands and laced our fingers together. "Because our rivals had claimed you. They said their top alpha wanted you as his own. That being the case, there was nothing I could do without starting an all-out-war. So, in order to protect myself, I kept you at arm's length. I thought maybe if I made you resent me it wouldn't hurt so bad."

I frowned. "But... no one ever 'claimed' me."

"I don't think they ever had the intention to. You're simply the chess piece they needed to start a rivalry. They knew that sooner or later, I would fight for you. And that time has finally come."

"So, you started a war because of me?"

He leaned forward like he was about to kiss me but then he stopped just before our lips could come together.

"Yeah, I wouldn't do that if I were you," Vern said.

"Huh?"

"I put some medicine on your lips," he explained. "It tastes horrible."

As soon as he pointed it out, I became aware of its bitterness. "Aw, why did you have to tell me?" I tried to get rid of it but it seemed permanently stuck to my lips.

Lyle chuckled under his breath.

I shot him a killer glare.

He rose to his feet. "I am sure that is more than enough for you to think about. Try and get some rest. When you awake, one of us will be right through that door."

The two of them helped ease me back into bed. I wanted to resist it but then the fatigue settled into my bones. My eyelids became heavy. There was nothing I could do to stop the wave of sleepiness. So, I embraced it and had some of the most wonderful dreams of my life.

Chapter 18 Lyle

I added a bit more kindling to the fire and watched it burned. The flames were a deep amber color, highlighted by the day's dying sun. Despite its warmth, I felt a chill. That chill, I knew, was the repercussion of the dread building up inside of me. Ari now knew the truth. How would she truly react? What would happen from this point forward? The uncertainty was chewing away at my sanity.

To curb my madness, I gathered up some cooking materials and started to work on dinner. As soon as the pot boiled, I added some stew meat and stirred it against the thickening vegetable broth.

"Cooking?" Vern appeared on the back porch of our hut.

"Shouldn't you be keeping an eye on her?" I said. I didn't bother to turn around and look at him. Instead, I busied myself with buttering a few cobs of corn and wrapping them with pieces of tin foil.

"She's fine. The poison is out of her system now. The elder assured me that she'll make a full recovery. In fact, she should be up and on her feet by this evening." He sauntered over and stole a piece of meat from the stew. Before I could stop him, he popped it into his mouth. "Mmm, this is some good cooking."

I scowled. "Leave me alone."

Vern sighed and sat down beside me. "Something is bothering you."

I turned away and poked at the chicken I had roasting on the fire. It was burning on one side so I slowly rotated it to cook evenly.

"You have to talk to me," Vern pressed. "If you cannot confide in your own beta then who else?"

I could tell that he wasn't going to let this go. My patience was wearing thin but nonetheless, I swept my tongue along my lips, preparing to explain myself. "If you must know, I'm nervous."

"Nervous?"

"Yes."

Vern laughed.

"What's so funny?" I snapped.

"The fact that you think being nervous is something you should be ashamed about."

"Isn't it?"

"Not at all." He rested a hand on my shoulder and squeezed it. "That just proves that you have a heart inside of that chest of yours and that you really care about this girl." He pointed his thumb at the hut. "It's not just about lust or desire. We're better than that. Ari is our mate and we're destined to cherish and love her."

It surprised me that Vern spoke with such leveled wisdom. He was usually the smart aleck who did nothing but crack jokes all the time. Very rarely did he take something seriously. I was glad this was one of those times.

"And you're scared that she isn't going to love us back but I think you're wrong there. She feels the tug of the mate just as strongly as we do. That's why she ran into the woods that night. She wanted to protect you even if she did not know it."

I allowed his words to settle. Maybe he was speaking the truth after all.

"Anyway, I should go take a bath. I smell."

My nostrils flared as I picked up the scent. "Jeez." I groaned as my stomach churned. He wasn't kidding. "I'm surprised you haven't woken up Ari with that smell. It's stronger than bath salts."

Vern laughed. "I guess I've been so preoccupied with taking care of her that I didn't stop to think of myself." He rubbed the back of his neck. "Anyway, I'll be down by the river for a while. Would you mind keeping an eye on her while I'm gone? If anything goes awry, send something to fetch me."

I nodded. "Go on. I'll take care of her."

He took one more look at the hut before walking away.

I got up and stretched my legs. To better hear her, I opened up the back door and then got back to my cooking. With most of it done, I started setting up the table. The day was much too wonderful to let it go to waste.

The tablecloth fluttered in the wind while the flames danced around the chicken, blackening it to perfection. The smell of it wafted into the air, making it thick with the mixture of spices I had used as seasoning. I was practically drooling by the time everything was said and done.

I sat down in front of my buffet of food, planning to devour the feast but the loneliness of it weighed on my shoulders. What was the point of all this food if I had no one to share it with?

Just then, one of the creaky floorboards caught my attention. I turned my head and saw Ari standing in the doorway. She wore nothing but one of my button-ups. Her hair was tussled from laying in bed all this time.

My jaw nearly hung agape. I no longer had an appetite for food – I had an appetite for that. All I wanted to do was sink my teeth into her breasts and watch the ecstasy wash over her face. From there, I'd run my tongue over every single inch of her body from tip to toe. But there was one place, in particular, that would get most of my attention – that lovely little honey pot of hers.

"Did you make all this?" Her question broke my lust-induced trance.

"Yes," I answered. "Would you like some?"

She nodded. "I'm famished. I guess passing out for a few days does that to a girl." It was good to hear that she could still laugh after her ordeal.

I got up and pulled out her chair. She blushed ever so slightly at my display at chivalry. Apparently, human men no longer believed in the practice. Idiots.

"Thank you." She whispered.

"Certainly," I returned. My lips were so close to her ear that I was tempted to give it a little nibble but I knew if I allowed myself the liberty, then one thing would lead to another and she was still much too weak to have me bending her over the table.

I returned to my chair and sliced through the chicken, taking a portion of the breast for myself.

"What would you like?"

"A wing, if that's okay."

I gave her both and piled her plate with a little bit of everything.

"I can't eat this much food!" She protested.

"I'm not asking you to."

As we enjoyed the food, neither one of us found the need to talk. We were perfectly content with enjoying each other's company.

I tried to make it as subtle as possible but I couldn't keep my eyes off of her. She was so breathtakingly beautiful that it was taking every ounce of my willpower to keep from pouncing on her. All I wanted to do was claim her as my own because I could no longer stand the idea that someone could swoop in and take her from me.

"This is delicious," she complimented. "I didn't know you were such a good cook."

"I enjoy it."

"Really?" She tilted her head to the side, causing some of her tangled curls to frame the side of her face. She was making it so much harder for me to control myself. "I don't mean to be rude but I always assumed that billionaires had people who cooked for them."

"I'm a dragon before I'm a billionaire."

She shook her head. "I still cannot believe that you're a dragon. It's hard for me to wrap my head around."

"Does it make you afraid?"

"Afraid?" She repeated as if she didn't recognize the word. "Not at all. If anything, it makes me feel safer." She paused and reached over the table where she took my hand in hers. "I'm no fool. I know I was followed that night and that you were the one to protect me."

"Technically, I had no right to interfere. The Aetos have a claim –"

"I don't care about that. They never consulted me about this claim of theirs so as far as I'm concerned, I have no obligation to abide by it." She stabbed one of her potatoes. "When really all I want..." she trailed off.

I squeezed her hand, waiting for an answer but it never came because Vern came bursting through the door, dripping wet from his recent bath. He offered a lopsided grin as he plopped down and joined us for dinner. I was well aware of the way Ari looked at him. Then, it hit me.

Perhaps she was only interested in one of us.

Chapter 19 Ari

In a way, I felt whole. Being with these men filled a hole in my heart I didn't know existed. It thumped with excitement as I heard the familiarity of their voices. It was almost like I had known them for years – maybe even in another life.

The smile on my face seemed bent on staying there permanently.

"Well, we should probably get you home."

"Home?" I repeated. Suddenly, the idea seemed so foreign. "But what if the Aetos show up? Now I'm not saying I'm a weakling but I'm pretty sure I couldn't fend off a bunch of dragons." Panic rose with my every word as I considered my abandonment. More than anything else, I didn't want to leave their sides. To do so, felt like I might lose a part of myself.

"Who said anything about abandoning you?" Vern lifted my chin and our eyes locked. "We'll stay the night to make sure you're safe."

"And why can't we stay here?"

"Because we are not mated," Lyle explained. "Our clan is sometimes used as a refuge for humans that have been injured due to our kind. For example, when you were poisoned, you had the right to treatment by the elders. Now that you are healed, you are required to leave."

"But why?"

"We are not mated and you have not received the blessing needed to become a clan's member."

I frowned and screwed up my eyebrows. In a way, it seemed like they didn't want me there. "So, what happens if we mate?"

Lyle looked like I had just punched him in the stomach.

"Then you would go through the acceptance ceremony and should you pass, you're a part of our dragon family." Vern stepped in, taking over where Lyle could no longer answer. "Don't worry about it." He said as if reading my mind. "It's not difficult. So long as you prove you love and honor the dragons you have mated then you'll pass with flying colors.

Love and honor, the words echoed through my head. Did I love these men? I was certainly attracted to them but I didn't want to confuse lust with love.

"Do you want to mate with us?" Lyle's eyes burned with expectation. That gaze was enough to pierce through to my very soul, revealing my true emotions.

"Yes," I answered without an ounce of hesitation. "I would."

His eyes widened. "Even after everything we have told you? Even after the way I treated you as a teenager? You still want us... both?"

It was strange to see the confident billionaire exposing his insecurities. Clearly, he thought I wasn't interested and the rejection was killing him inside.

"Yes, I want you both." I blushed slightly as my mind conjured up images of what that would look like. Was my bed even big enough to hold all three of us? "But..."

"You'd like some time?" Vern guessed.

"How are you doing that?"

"Doing what?"

"Taking the words right out of my mouth," I said.

He chuckled and offered me a shrug. "Honestly, I don't know but I've always had a knack for it. I do it to Lyle all the time."

Lyle nodded in agreement. "It's true. Rather annoying at times when he fails to let me talk."

"I see," I said with a chuckle. It was amusing to see the two men clashing together. Despite their front, it was obvious they cared deeply for one another. Perhaps that is what allowed them to share a partner without jealousy. "Anyway, if we're set to go home then I wouldn't mind getting there sooner rather than later. I really need a bath."

"Is this bath of yours big enough for three?" Vern grinned.

Lyle jabbed his side. "Vern." He chastised. "She says she wants time. Don't go off teasing her now."

"It's alright," I whispered. Truth be told, sharing a bath with these men seemed like a dream come true. But, at the same time, I didn't want to rush things. It seemed if I accepted their offer to mate, it would turn out to be the biggest decision of my life. Things would no longer be the same and I wasn't sure whether I was ready for that.

"Here." Lyle handed me some fresh clothing. "One of the clan sisters left it here for you to wear when you recovered. I doubt you want to continue wearing my shirt. It gets a little nippy at night, especially on the back of a dragon." As he said the word 'nippy' his eyes dropped to my chest. It was then that I noticed that my chest could barely contain itself within the thin material of his shirt. The girls were both on full display for either one of them to ogle at.

Had it been anyone else, I probably would have slapped them but with Lyle and Vern, things were different. They didn't feel like a couple of pervs trying to take advantage of me. Instead, they felt like my sexy protectors.

So, their wandering eyes only worked to turn me on. The heat blazed between my legs and grew hotter by the minutes. I knew I wanted to wait but how long would I hold out against this feeling?

"Ari?"

I blinked. "Sorry." I took the clothes from his outstretched hand. Our fingers brushed against one another and I felt a spark which led the current through my arm and into my heart. I gasped, sucking in air through my teeth. At that moment, I could see my future. It involved these two men and without them, everything would turn to gray.

"Are you alright?" Vern asked as he placed his hand on mine.

Just as with Lyle, a spark flew through my system. My future became clearer – crisper. I needed these men. Now, I had to find the courage to tell them.

I fidgeted from foot to foot. It did not help. So, in the end, I retreated to my temporary room and changed into the outfit I had been given. They were pretty normal looking clothes – just a pair of jeans and a t-shirt. I don't know what I expected but it certainly wasn't this.

The fabric of the jeans was nice and soft, hugging all my curves to perfection. For a good portion of my life, I had resented those curves but with the look of hunger I got from my two future mates, I knew they found them attractive. That thought alone was enough to have my confidence rocketing through the roof.

"Ready?" Lyle asked once I returned to the kitchen table.

"Yes, I think so."

He nodded and off he went through the back door. I followed with Vern flanking my behind – literally.

I could feel his stare so I gave him a bit of a show by swaying my hips from side to side. I giggled when he tripped over his own two feet.

We arrived at a large clearing. All of a sudden, Lyle was replaced by a gigantic dragon. "Whoa..." I whispered aloud, unable to believe my eyes. "You look just like a real dragon."

"That's because he is a real dragon," Vern whispered against my ear. His hand brushed against the top of my ass as he stepped aside and called forth his own wings. "Can you transform like that too?" I asked.

He shook his head. "No. That's an honor reserved for alphas. I'm stuck with these wings."

"I still think they're pretty cool," I said when I heard the disappointment in his voice. "Just don't tell Lyle," I winked.

When I looked up, Lyle's face was right there. His golden eyes were almost as big as I was. On second thought, I think they were bigger. He blinked and a leathery lid crossed horizontally across his eyeball.

"Okay... that's a little weird." Before I could say anything else, he nuzzled me with his snout and a second later, I figured out that he wanted me to climb his head. It felt like I was climbing a mountain. As I went higher and higher, I reminded myself to keep from looking down.

By some miracle, I reached the nape of his neck. There, I found a good place to sit and hold on to. In a way, it felt like it had been made for me.

I wanted to brace myself but we were already soaring through the clouds. Adrenaline pumped through my veins. I screamed with glee as the wind whipped through my hair and threw it over my shoulders.

"Exhilarating, isn't it?" Vern swooped in beside me. "Lyle is the biggest dragon in this part of the hemisphere. Not many people can boast they've been on his back."

"Wait, has there been others?" I asked as a pang of jealousy shot through my heart. I hadn't stopped to consider that perhaps these men had enjoyed other women. The implications of their past and all that they had done loomed over my happiness like a dark cloud.

"Only one," he answered.

I frowned, trying to picture what she might have looked like.

"Me."

"What?"

"Me. I'm the only other person."

"Are you being serious?"

Vern nodded. "He doesn't like it very much. He says that the thought makes him feel like a pack mule."

"So, am I making him uncomfortable?"

"If you could see his face right now, I'd say he's happier than a hog in mud."

Abruptly, a barbed tail came flying out of nowhere and it knocked Vern right out of the sky. Lyle rumbled underneath me and that's when I realized he was laughing.

Vern reappeared a second later. "Was that really necessary?"

I hid my mouth behind my hand. I didn't want to upset Vern by laughing at his expense, but I just couldn't help myself.

He glared, hands on his hips but behind that, I could see a hint of amusement. He wasn't really mad.

"So, when do we get to my house?"

"We're already there," Vern answered.

I dared to look down and saw Lyle flapping his powerful wings as he made his descent into my backyard.

"Uh... what happens if one of the neighbors happen to look out the window and sees a giant dragon touching down?" If people caught wind that dragons were real, I had the sinking feeling that it wouldn't end well for their population. Lyle and Vern would probably be taken away to some government facility for testing. I shivered at the thought.

"No worries," Vern said. "When we are together, there's a sort of magic that makes us invisible to humans. Their mind tricks them into thinking they saw something else. For example, they might think Lyle is just passing fog. Or, if they do happen to see us, they'll usually convince themselves into thinking it was just a figment of their imagination."

"Right..." I said. "There's a lot that goes into this dragon stuff, huh?"

"I suppose it's complicated to a newcomer. I've never really thought about it."

"It makes my head spin. I'm sitting on a dragon and its still hard to believe that you guys are real. I keep thinking I'm going to wake up and find out that this is all a dream." I paused. "And it terrifies me because I do not want this to end."

Abruptly, Lyle transformed into a man. I fell from a great height only to land safely in his arms. He smiled down at me. "It isn't going to end," he said with sincerity. Without a further word, he walked into my home.

I was made acutely aware of how messy it was. The sink was piled with dirty dishes. The floor needed to be swept. Why hadn't I tidied up the place?

To my surprise, Lyle did not consider his surroundings. He walked with a clear purpose straight to my bedroom. How he knew where it was, I didn't dare to ask. I was much more concerned with the feeling of his arms wrapped around my body, keeping me safe and sound.

I rested my head against his chest and all of a sudden, fatigue washed over me.

"You haven't fully recovered," Vern explained as Lyle laid me down. Gently, he ran his fingers through my hair, pushing it away from my face. "The medicine we gave you is very powerful and has sedative side effects. I wouldn't be surprised if you feel sluggish for the next couple of days."

The two men tucked me in. They headed for the door.

"Wait!" I called out before they could leave. "I know I said I wanted to wait for us to mate... but do you think you could stay with me?"

They exchanged a quick glance before nodding their heads in agreement. They slipped into bed on either side of my body. Instantly, I felt like I was being engulfed by a furnace. I melted against the heat and found peace washing over me. Here, in their arms, nothing could hurt me.

I nuzzled against Vern while Lyle held me from behind.

It was perfect.

Maybe a little too perfect.

***

I do not know when I fell asleep, but I do know when I woke up. A searing pain tore through my chest, just above my left breast. It sizzled against my flesh, choking me with the smell of something rotten. I tried to scream but no noise escaped my throat.

My body thrashed with the agony.

What was happening to me?

"Ari!" Lyle exclaimed with alarm.

"They've imprinted her," Vern responded, his voice somber. He rushed over to the window. "Those bastards!" He pounded the glass with his fist and it rattled against the frame. "They're going to pay for this."

While Vern was busy losing his temper, Lyle was trying to calm me down. He ran his thumb across my cheek. "Shh…" he whispered. "It's going to be okay. It'll pass." He kissed the top of my forehead. "Just try to think of something else – something that makes you happy."

Despite his advice, the pain continued. I whimpered as it transformed into a stabbing torture like someone had a dagger and kept thrusting it into my heart over and over again. "What is happening?" I cried out, my voice barely a whisper.

"The Aetos imprinted on you without your consent. It is a dastardly deed as it pains the woman like nothing else." Vern paced the length of the bed.

"Does that mean…?" I asked with dread. "We can no longer be together?" Tears welled up in my eyes. This was my punishment for waiting too long. Now I was never going to have the men that I wanted.

Lyle was about to say something when a loud crash rang through my ears.

A tall, well-built man stood by the broken window, a devilish grin on his face.

Lyle held me so tightly that I thought my ribs would shatter.

"I believe you are holding what is rightfully mine," said the man.

"Rot in hell!" Lyle passed me off to Vern. Once I was safe in his arms, Lyle stepped forward, fists tight and ready. "Because I don't think you have the guts to tell me that to my face."

The man swung a dagger but Lyle was quick to avoid it. He clipped the intruder's legs and brought him to the ground. They both snarled, sharp teeth snapping at one another. I flinched at every blow that was given.

Vern shielded me against his chest so I wouldn't have to look but I couldn't keep from watching the fight. I prayed with all my might that Lyle would win and that there would be some kind of solution to this horrible nightmare.

Suddenly, the Aetos member held out his hand and again I was inflicted with agonizing pain. I fell to my knees, shaking. The pain was so much that I couldn't hold the contents of my stomach. I doubled over, getting on my hands and knees.

"You're going to pay for that." Lyle snarled from across the room.

Snap.

Through a blurry sight, I saw the man's arm hanging at a peculiar angle. My stomach twisted into an even tighter knot.

The hatred on Lyle's face frightened me. I was sure he was going to end it right then and there. I braced myself but the Aetos member managed to weasel his way from Lyle's tight hold. He turned on his heels and fled like a coward.

"Don't," Vern said when Lyle made the move to follow the assailant. "We have to help her," he added.

Lyle crossed the room and rested his enormous hand on my back, supporting me.

"Is there no way to make this stop?" It was difficult to breath when it felt like someone had broken my sternum in an attempt to rip out my heart. "It hurts so bad..." I whimpered as I bared my teeth, trying to stay strong. "Please..." I begged. If this continued on for much longer, I was certain I would die. "I..." My shoulders sagged. "All I want is to be with you. Don't let them take me away."

Chapter 20 Lyle

I took her hand and squeezed it. "There is one way." I hesitated and chose my words very carefully. "But it comes at a risk."

"Anything," she croaked.

"If you truly love someone else, it'll break the imprint," Vern spoke in a quiet whisper. "But, if there is any doubt, you will die."

She gulped.

"So, Ari, the question stands." I cupped her face in my hands and turned it so she was forced to look at me. "Do you love us?"

"Yes." With what little strength she had left, she leaned forward and planted a kiss against my lips.

At that moment, I felt complete. Unable to resist, I wrapped my arm around her waist and pulled her close until our bodies had melded together as one. Only then did I return her fevered kiss with a passion of my own.

My tongue slipped into her mouth, tangling against hers.

She clawed at my clothes, desperate for more.

"Ahem." Vern cleared his throat. I ignored him. He would just have to wait a little longer.

Lust flowed through my veins like molten lava.

I pushed her onto the ground and pinned her underneath my body as the kiss continued. I bit down on her bottom lip and tugged on it until I heard her moan. I did not give her a moment's rest as I attacked her mouth with my own. I breathed her in but it still wasn't enough to satisfy.

My lungs burned so I pulled away ever so slightly. The last thing I wanted to do was suffocate her. She sucked in much-needed air. There was a bright smile on her face.

"How's the pain?" I whispered as I tucked a strand of hair behind her ear.

"It's fading away but it's still there." Her eyes glanced over at Vern. "Could it be…?"

Vern answered her with a mischievous smirk. "Step aside." He pushed me off and took my place. He was much less aggressive but the passion was clear. Their bodies grinded together with a silent need.

Knowing where this would lead, I started to take off my clothes. First came the tie; I threw it aside and it landed on one of the bed posters. How convenient. Perhaps I could use it to my advantage later on in our love play. Sometimes, adding a blindfold could really spice things up. My thoughts wandered as I thought of the countless possibilities. Tonight was only the beginning. If Ari was to be our mate, then we'd have plenty of time to explore and experiment.

When I had taken off my shirt, I noticed that Vern had worked his way down to her breasts. His tongue rolled around her puckered nipples, flicking them back and forth. His other hand kneaded her sensitive flesh until her head rolled back with bliss.

"How's the pain now?" I asked as my hand slid underneath her jeans and into her panties. She was extremely wet and getting even wetter by the second.

"Gone."

Knowing that my cue to have at it, I slipped my fingers between her folds. I teased her clit, rolling it back and forth until she bucked her hips into the air, begging for more.

Her moan was muffled as Vern returned to her lips. My cock sprang to life as I smelled her excitement in the air. I could no longer wait. This woman would be mine.

I pushed my middle finger inside of her. At first, it was just the tip. My intention was to drive her insane. I wanted her screaming my name by the end of the night.

Vern rose to his feet and started to undress. Ari watched him with an expression painted in excitement and lust. I took this distraction and surprised her by shoving in two of my fingers knuckle deep. She screamed, back arching. I didn't give her a moment of rest before I started moving them hard and fast.

She was so wet that she had started to leak through her panties. It was time I remedied that problem. I got between her legs and unbuttoned her pants. Slowly, I took them off, gliding my fingers along her silken skin. Once they were off, I trailed kisses along her thighs, getting closer and closer to her mound.

"Lyle..." she whispered as she reached forward and took hold of my hair.

I offered her a smirk before I took her thong between my teeth. With a flick of my head, I ripped it off her body. It went flying across the room where Vern caught it. "Mmm." He mused. "Someone's nice and wet. If I had to guess, someone wants us. Don't you think?"

With her pussy right in front of me, I didn't bother to answer. Instead, I attacked her with my tongue. She was sweeter than I could have imagined. I dove deeper, trying to taste her from the source.

She pulled at my hair trying to get me to go a little faster so that's exactly what I did. I twisted my tongue this way and that way while lapping up every last drop of nectar she had to offer me. Hungry with lust, my fingers dug into her thighs in my attempt to feast further within her.

I held her down when she tried to squirm.

She moaned as I paused to tease her clit. I flicked it back and forth before sucking on it.

"Please..." she begged.

I continued my assault, determined to make her cum before we reached the bed. So, I ate her out even faster. My tongue became a blur as it shot in and out of her.

She nearly ripped the hair right off my head as her body shook with pleasure. I could tell by the look on her face that she had just experienced one of the best orgasms of her life.

Only then did I stop and pull away.

"Wow…" she breathed, panting for air. "You're quite… skilled."

"You haven't seen anything yet."

Chapter 21 Ari

My head was spinning. No one had ever made me feel that good before. A deep, tingling sensation still coursed through my veins, making it hard to focus on anything else.

Between my legs, a puddle was forming. Jeez, I didn't even think it was possible to get this wet.

Suddenly, Lyle picked me up in his capable hands and laid me down on the bed. He cupped my cheeks in his hand and looked at me like I was the only girl in the world. I shivered with delight as his lips joined mine. It was like we were a couple of puzzle pieces coming together for the first time – a perfect fit.

His tongue was demanding and aggressive. It wrestled with mine until it had dominance over my mouth.

All too soon, he pulled away and turned me around so I was on my hands and knees. I wiggled my ass, trying to entice the dragon. He responded by smacking my left ass cheek. I wasn't expecting it. I jerked forward and that's when I came face to face with Vern's cock. He had been lounging there the whole time, enjoying the show between me and his partner.

"Reckon you might want a taste of your own," he said with this sly little grin on his face. "Go ahead."

I couldn't resist. I crawled forward and greeted him with my tongue. Now, I'm not very experienced with such things but there was something about his cock that made it impossible to resist. So, I followed my instincts and they guided me through the motions.

"Mmm, that's it." He praised me as he grabbed a fistful of my hair and pushed me further along his tip.

I tightened my lips and swirled my tongue all around the sensitive head. It seemed to throb underneath my attention and I liked that.

To get closer, I leaned forward while gripping the base of his shaft in a tight grip.

"Move your hand, baby girl," he instructed in a feral purr.

I did as he asked. I found his length was nice and slick from all the licking I had done beforehand. For that reason, I was able to glide up and down without any resistance. He seemed to grow bigger and bigger with each passing second. As it stood, I had no idea how he was going to fit inside of me. Surely, he'd rip me right in two.

That's when I felt Lyle creeping up behind me. His own raging member slipped between my ass cheeks. My eyes widened. If Vern was big, Lyle was massive.

His fingertips danced along the length of my spine. Once he reached my lower back, he leaned down and kissed my ass. His lips felt divine. I almost forgot what I was doing but Vern regained my attention when he started to guide my head up and down his length.

I tried to accommodate his size but after a few inches, I was already gagging. Vern didn't seem to mind. He just tightened his grip and kept on going. I dug my nails into his thighs as I started to deep throat him as best I could.

It was hard to focus with Lyle probing around my ass. His fingers were ice-cold when they found my puckered asshole. He rubbed my back to get me to calm down before applying pressure. My toes curled and I tried to pull away by rocking forward.

Vern took his chance and held me down. His every inch was down my throat, making it impossible for me to breath. I begged him with my eyes and he finally let me go. I pulled away, gasping for air but a second later, I was back on his dick. I just couldn't help myself. There was something about these men that unlocked a side of me that I barely recognized. It was like I had transformed into some kind of a vixen. I just couldn't get enough.

Suddenly, Lyle shoved a finger deep inside my hole. I screamed, sending vibrations through Vern's length. He groaned with pleasure and pushed his hips into the air. His thrusts continued until he was effectively fucking my mouth. Trying to please him even further, I reached for his balls. They were nice and smooth. I fondled them between my fingers, my touch unbelievably gentle.

"Mmm, baby." He released my hair.

I pulled away from his cock and ran my tongue all the way down his length until I reached his balls. There, my tongue did a bit of exploring. I searched his every inch until he was clawing at the sheets. Smirking, I leaned down even further and took one of his balls into my mouth, sucking on it.

Vern sucked in air through his teeth.

"Careful," Lyle warned. "You wouldn't want to make him blow too quickly." He whispered against my ear as a second lubed up finger penetrated my ass. "There's still a lot more to go. The night is only beginning." His fingers hooked inside me, finding a pleasure point I didn't know existed. Lyle targeted it until my legs started to shake.

He grabbed me by the hips so that my ass was in the air and kept me in that position as he added yet another finger. All three worked to stretch out my tightness. I moaned and whimpered as a mixture of pleasure and pain went through my body.

Then, just as things were getting really good, he stopped. With a yank of my hair, he had me laying on my back.

Vern rolled out of the way and Lyle took his spot. "Come here." He growled.

So, I crawled on top of me. He immediately started to finger my pussy, finding that it was even wetter than it had been before. A satisfied smile painted his face as he pulled me toward his massive cock. I couldn't believe how big it was. There was no way it could fit inside of me and yet, that's exactly what I wanted. If I couldn't have his girth stretching me nice and wide, I was bound to lose my mind.

"Beg for it." He tugged on my hair, forcing my head back. Doing so exposed my neck which he attacked with those fiery lips of his. "Tell me how much you want me."

"Please..." I started. "I want to feel your cock inside me. I want to milk it for every last drop. I can't stand all this teasing. I need you. I need Vern. Both of you working as one. I want to feel stuffed and when you're done, I don't want to walk straight for a week."

Vern positioned himself behind me, the tip of his cock lined up with my asshole. I held my breath, waiting for him to penetrate deep inside me but it never came. Instead, Lyle rested his hands on my hips and pulled me forward. He coated his length with my juices before nodding his head. "Very well." He reached forward and cupped one of my breasts against his palm. "Come and get it."

It took me a moment to realize what he wanted. I blushed slightly. He wanted me to take control but I felt horribly inexperienced. I had never done anything like this before. Nevertheless, my lust guided me forward. Once I was ready, I lifted myself up before slowly lowering myself onto his length.

I gasped the second his tip popped into my pussy. He was so big and this was only the beginning. He was bound to get thicker, the lower I went. I braced myself as my hole stretched around his girth.

"You're so tight..." he growled.

"And you're so big..." I rested my hands on his chest to support myself. By doing so, I was able to impale myself completely. I paused to catch my breath and that's when Vern made his move.

It took me by surprise. One second, he was teasing me with his hand and the next, he was balls deep inside of me. I screamed thinking I would rip right in two. I arched my back, toes curling with the sensation.

The men did not spare a moment. As soon as they were fully inside, they started to slide back and forth, building up the perfect rhythm.

I could barely stand it. With my pussy already sensitive from my initial orgasm, I didn't know how much of this I could take before I lost my mind.

Vern quickened his pace as he reached around my waist and found my clit. His thumb moved in circles, around and around. My thighs shook as fire exploded between them. As much as I wanted to, I couldn't hold back the orgasm. It ripped right through me, leaving me breathless.

But still, they did not stop. Lyle pounded into me even as my pussy quivered around his length.

Meanwhile, Vern was fucking me like a madman. His balls kept on slapping against Lyle's, the sound echoing through my room. There was something so carnal about it that it left me lightheaded with desire.

I tried to move and contribute to our lovemaking but the men were in complete control. I was simply their willing little puppet.

Soon, I lost count of my climaxes. It all just felt too good. I shook like a leaf every time they rocked into my body. My throat had grown raw from all the screaming and moaning. I was loving every minute of it.

And then, I felt Vern go rigid. His cock twitched inside of me before he pulled out and something warm shot across my back and most of my ass. He sighed and collapsed on the other side of the bed, cock still as hard as a flag pole.

A second later, Lyle flipped the tables. He pinned my wrists above my head as he pounded into me. The bed was rocking so hard that I was sure it would break. There was this animalistic look on his face.

I screamed his name and that's when it happened. He flooded my pussy with his cum. I moaned and sunk into the pillows. "Wow..."

He growled and nuzzled the side of my neck, nipping it with his teeth. "You're ours."

A deep, almost burning sensation arose just above my heart. That pain was quickly replaced with a sense of euphoria as a beautiful tattoo looking mark appeared. It depicted two dragons intertwined at the tail, one of them spewing a mouthful of fire towards my right breast.

"No one can ever take you away from us," Vern whispered as he ran his fingers through my hair. "We'll keep you safe."

I smiled and kissed them both. "This is crazy, but I think it's the best decision I've ever made."

Chapter 22 Vern

I woke up to find that Ari was no longer in bed with us. A feeling of panic surged inside my chest. Immediately, I rolled out of bed and sprang to my feet. Lyle continued to snore, nearly shaking the house's very foundation.

My eyes became serpentine as I honed my senses. Her scent was everywhere but I picked up the most recent trail and followed it to the kitchen. There, I found an open package of crackers with half of them missing. I grabbed the other half before heading outside.

Ari was rocking herself on the swing chair, a blanket wrapped around her shoulders. "Is everything alright?" I asked.

"Sorry, I couldn't sleep. I hope I didn't wake you."

I sat down beside her and pulled her into my embrace. "It's cold out here. You'll catch something if you stay."

"Just a little longer," she said as she rested her head on my chest. Together, we watched the stars while I rubbed her back.

"Are you sure everything is okay?"

Ari nibbled on her bottom lip. "It's just a little scary to think how much my life will change from this moment forward. It's not like I can go back to living a normal life when I've just had sex with a couple of dragons." She reached for her chest and outlined her mating mark. "I don't regret what we did. I know it was the right decision but that doesn't make it easy."

"I know." I kissed the top of her head. "But I promise you that Lyle and I will try to make it as painless as possible. We can take things slow. That's why I pulled out."

"Huh?"

"Had I climaxed inside of you, you would have been pregnant right now," he explained. "Dragons have a 100% fertility rate but both partners must orgasm inside the female."

"This dragon stuff really is complicated..."

Suddenly, her phone started to ring.

She looked down at it. "My friend, Becky."

"Go ahead, answer it."

"But what do I tell her?"

"Whatever you want. The truth is the hardest. A lie is easier."

She frowned at my advice. "Helpful."

I shrugged.

She answered the call, "Hello?"

While I couldn't distinguish the exact words, I would tell that her friend was worried. After all, Ari had disappeared for a couple of days. Ari soothed her with a made-up story about hiking in the woods. From the sound of it, her friend wasn't very convinced.

"I'll catch up with you later," she said before hanging up.

"You know, if you trust her, we can always bring her back to the clan. There are plenty of dragons looking for mates. Who knows, she might find the one."

"She'll lose her mind if she finds out that dragons are real."

"We thought you'd do the same but here you are."

Silence settled in around us. I didn't feel the need to break it so I tapped the ground with my foot, rocking us back and forth.

Overhead, the stars glittered like a sea full of diamonds.

Soon enough, I picked up on Ari's gentle breathing. She had fallen asleep. I picked her up and carried her into the bedroom. Gently, I laid her down on top of Lyle who was quick to wrap his arms around her. "Is everything alright?" He asked. "She feels cold."

"She spent some time outside," I said as I slipped under the covers. "Apparently, she couldn't sleep. I'm not surprised. This must be a lot for her to take in."

Lyle nodded as he played with her hair. "Anything else?"

"She has a friend she's worried about. They're particularly close."

"And she's afraid of losing that friend?"

"Yes. It would seem so."

"Perhaps she can find someone within the clan. They could become clan sisters."

"That's what I told her but she doesn't seem too thrilled by the idea. She thinks her friend will freak out if she finds out the truth."

"Have you met her before? This friend, I mean."

"Not that I know of." I pulled out my phone and checked Ari's social media. There, I found her friend's list. It wasn't a very extensive one. Ari, it seemed, wasn't the kind of person to clutter her life with unnecessary drama. "Hmm... no Becky here," I said aloud and kept scrolling.

"Maybe it's a nickname for Rebecca," Lyle suggested.

"Good thinking." I got down to the Rs and there she was. Her profile picture was one of her and Ari at a county fair. They both had bright smiles on their faces. "It seems she works at the local thrift store. Maybe I'll drop by there one of these days and see if she wouldn't be a suitable match for one of our clan brothers."

"Is she single?"

"That's what her status says."

"Alright." Lyle yawned.

"Seems like our new mate took a lot out of you." I teased. "I have never seen you work up such a sweat. At one point, I thought you were hell-bent on breaking this bed."

He gave me a sheepish look. "What can I say? We have the sexiest mate on the planet. It would have been a crime if I hadn't rocked her world."

I chuckled. "You have a point there."

"It feels so good to finally hold her in my arms. I always thought we'd stay enemies – that she would hate me forever."

"You'd be surprised what the heart is capable of forgiving."

He sighed. "Sometimes I regret how much of an asshole I was. There was no need for me to be so harsh with her."

"There's no point in mourning the past. You did what you thought you needed to do to protect yourself."

"But I didn't consider what she needed – what was best for her."

"Well, you can do that now," I said. "And I'll hold you accountable because she's my mate too and if you ever hurt her again, I'll have your head on a silver platter."

He laughed so hard that Ari woke up with this disoriented look on her face. "Huh? What's happening? Is that an earthquake?"

Now it was my time to laugh. "An earthquake? No. That's just Lyle."

She looked down and her cheeks reddened. "When did I get up here?"

Lyle held her a little tighter. "Vern brought you to bed but he made a big mistake handing you over because I'm never letting you go!"

"Hey!" I protested. "That's not fair."

"Life isn't fair." He shot back. "She's mine now."

"Boys, boys." Ari held up her hands. "There's plenty of me to go around."

"Is that so?" I raised my eyebrow in question. "In that case..."

"...Shall we start round two?" Lyle finished my sentence for me and together we pounced on our beautiful partner.

Chapter 23 Ari

The following morning.

For some reason, I had never gotten around to furnishing my room with curtains. So, every morning, I was rudely awakened by the morning sun. It filtered through the window panes and concentrated its brightness on my face.

I rolled over and nuzzled my face against Vern's smooth chest. He smelled like a fresh shower. I breathed it in while running my fingertips along his abs. He stirred slightly but continued to sleep. "I guess I wore you guys out," I said with a chuckle as I slowly made my way out of bed. I didn't make it very far before Lyle clamped his arms around my body.

His hold was so tight that I could barely breathe. "Lyle..." I croaked but he did not respond. Just like Vern, he was deep in the land of slumber.

I ran my hands along the tautness of his forearms. Lyle was a beast made of pure muscle. I had to wonder how long he spent in the gym working on his physique. My mind followed that train of thought and conjured up the image of him pumping iron, sweat pouring down his sexy body. Mmm.

My stomach growled with hunger. As much as I wanted to lay with these men all day long, I needed to get something into my system. So, I lifted his arm and shimmied myself free from his grasp. Once I was up on my feet, I became aware of the draft. I hadn't felt it while laying in bed because I was buffered by two incredible space heaters. But now I felt the wind whipping through the broken window. It stung against my cheeks.

I hugged myself, recalling the pain I had felt. What would have happened if my mates hadn't been around to protect me? The Aetos would have taken me away...

Unable to stand the thought, I shook it away. From the back of a chair, I grabbed a bathrobe and threw it on. I tightened the sash around my waist as I made my way down the stairs.

In the kitchen, I checked the fridge for ingredients. I wanted to surprise the dragons with some breakfast. "Hmm..." I clicked my tongue to the roof of my mouth. "What to make? What to make?" Truth be told, I'm not a very good cook. Half the time, I'm at risk of burning my whole house to the ground. Still, I couldn't let that stop me.

I was just about to crack my first egg over a warm skillet when there came a knock on the door. I turned off the stove and went over to answer it. I rose onto my tippy toes and peeked through the peephole to find Becky standing there with a box of donuts.

"Open up. I know you're there," she said when I hesitated. Lying to her over the phone was easy enough but doing it in person was a whole other matter. "Or I'll be forced to eat all these donuts by myself."

My stomach growled in protest. "Do you have Boston Cream?"

"Of course, I do." She answered. "What kind of friend would I be if I left those behind?"

The door swung back and I snatched up the box.

"Jeez." Becky shook her head as she followed me inside. "If I didn't know any better, I'd say you were a pregnant woman."

"I suppose I worked up an appetite." I picked up my donut of choice and bit into the creamy center.

"What have you been doing?" Becky asked with a look of suspicion.

"Me." Vern stood in the door, posed like a GQ model. Thankfully, he had put his pants back on. They hung precariously on his hips, teasing me with the smoothness of his torso.

Becky's jaw hung agape.

"And me too."

Her jaw now threatened to hit the floor as she saw Lyle wearing nothing but a pair of boxer briefs. They left very little to the imagination.

"Wait a second," she glanced at me and then at the two handsome men standing before her. "You mean you banged both of them? Like at the same time?"

My face was red as a tomato. This wasn't exactly the manner in which I wanted to tell my best friend about my relationship.

"What wild club did you guys go to last night and why wasn't I invited?"

"We didn't go to a club." I tried to explain but she held up her hand stopping me.

"I don't believe it. Somehow, you managed to bag two breathtaking hunks and I can't even manage to flirt with the grocery clerk," she huffed. "I thought you were supposed to help a sister out."

"Well, you see, it's kind of complicated."

"Clearly."

"We're dragons," Vern said without skipping a beat.

"Dragons?" Becky repeated. "You know, never mind. I don't want to be dragged into whatever crazy roleplay you guys are into. I think I should probably leave. It seems y'all are busy at the moment."

"No, wait." I grabbed her by the wrist. "He's telling the truth."

"Have you lost your mind? Dragons aren't real, Ari. Now I don't know what kind of drugs you were taking last night but these guys aren't dragons. I can promise you that."

Lyle stepped forward and his wings came shooting out of his shoulders. "Do you believe us now?"

And that's when Becky fainted. Luckily, I was able to catch her before she could bang her head on the ground. "I told you she would freak out." I shot at Vern. "This was a bad idea. We should have eased her into it. You probably gave her a heart attack or something!"

Lyle simply picked her up and carried her over to the couch. Vern grabbed a kitchen cloth and doused it underneath the tap. He placed it on her forehead. "She'll be fine."

"How can you be so sure?" I asked as I fanned her face with a nearby book.

Before he could answer, she started to come through. She blinked. "Ari..."

"Yes, it's me." I took her hand and squeezed it. "What happened? I had the craziest dream that you were shacking up with a couple of dragons."

I gulped. "That's because... I am."

Slowly, she sat up. She ran her fingers through her hair before her eyes wandered over to Lyle who still had his wings exposed. "This is crazy."

"I know it's difficult to believe but I promise you that this is real."

"How?"

"Dragons have been a species for thousands of years. Our numbers have dwindled significantly. To save ourselves, we learned to blend in with humans. So, with time, the humans thought us extinct and we became a legend." Vern explained as he nibbled on a chocolate frosted donut.

"So, you're telling me that there could be a bunch of dragons just walking around town right now."

"That's correct."

She got up and started to pace back and forth. "And how did you get involved in all this?" She stopped to look at me. "I mean, what convinced you that it would be a good idea to have a relationship with two – not one – but two – dragons?"

"Well, that's just how they operate."

"Oh, of course it is." Becky threw up her hands. "I didn't know dragons were fans of threesomes. Is there something wrong with monogamy?"

"Nothing at all," Lyle interjected. "And for most species, it works but for dragons, having two male partners allows further protection for offspring."

"Offspring?" Becky bellowed. "Please don't tell me you're pregnant."

"Please, you're taking this out of proportion." I took her by the shoulders but she pulled away.

"I think I have a right to react this way. You had a threesome with dragons!" She held her head in her hands. "Now that's a sentence I never thought I would say." She paused. "Have you lost your mind?"

"Um... well... have you seen them?" I said in a meek whisper. "It's kind of hard to say no when two Greek Gods want to take you to bed."

She froze in place, considering my words. Suddenly, she turned around, eyes wandering over the bodies of my boyfriends. "Do all dragons look like you? I mean, physically?"

"For the most part," Lyle answered. "We are required to train from a young age so we can protect our clan."

"Clan?"

"It's where we live." Vern was on his third donut but even as he stuffed his face, he managed to answer her.

"So, there's a lot more of you?"

"About fifty or so."

"And how many are available...?"

"Oh, so now you're interested." I poked her side.

"Hey, you said it yourself, these two are hot as hell. If there's a chance I can hook up with someone half as hot as they are, I'll be one lucky girl."

"I can tell you that mating with dragons is one of the highest honors," Lyle said. "We are proud people and we choose our women very carefully. For that reason, we cherish and protect them. You'd be in very good hands."

"I'll be the judge of that," Becky said. "Now when do I get to meet these so-called dragons."

"Right now, if you'd like to accompany us. Ari has to receive her blessing from the elders so she can carry our children." Vern licked his fingers of frosting.

"Children? Seriously?"

I nodded. "You know I've always wanted kids."

"Aren't you moving a little too fast?" She asked, suddenly serious. "I mean, you've only known them for a short period of time."

I shook my head. "It's a feeling that I can't really explain to you."

She studied my face, her brows knitted together in confusion.

"But I just know that this is the right thing to do."

She rested her hand on top of mine. "If that's how you feel then I will support you every step of the way."

Chapter 24 Lyle

"We should get going. The blessing ceremony occurs at high noon," I said. "And the sooner Ari receives her blessing, the sooner we can start a family." I never thought I'd be able to say those words. They filled me with such happiness.

The girls followed us into the yard where I did a full transformation. Becky was nearly knocked off her feet with surprise. "Whoa... he looks like he belongs in a movie or something!" She inched forward. "Can I touch him?"

I nodded and craned my neck so my head was right in front of her. With a trembling hand, she reached forward and pressed her palm against my snout.

Once she pulled away, I picked up Ari and she climbed into place.

"I can't believe this is actually happening..." Becky mumbled underneath her breath.

Ari held out her hand and helped her friend.

"All set?" Vern asked.

"Mhm." Ari had a bright smile on her face and it only got wider as we took off towards the clouds.

"Holy shit!" Becky screamed as she held on for dear life. "Can you tell him to slow the fuck down?"

Ari laughed. "Faster!"

"This isn't funny!" Becky protested.

By the sound of it, Becky was on the verge of shitting her pants and Ari was getting quite a kick out of tormenting her friend. Figuring I would add fuel to the fire, I swooped down low before doing a spiraling twist toward the heavens.

"He's trying to kill us!" Becky dug her nails into my scales.

"He's just having some fun." Ari patted the side of my neck in a sign of thanks.

All too soon, our fun was over. I touched down. Becky was quick to scramble to the ground. Her knees knocked together as she struggled to stand. Her face was pale and her eyes were close to bulging out of their sockets. "You know what? I think that dating a dragon might not be the best thing for me. I don't really think they're my type."

"You're already here, you might as well give it a shot." Ari dragged her forward.

"Do you think this was a good idea?" I whispered over at Vern once I transformed into my human form.

"Absolutely. I haven't laughed this much in a long time."

"I wonder how the elders are going to react." I thought aloud.

"I doubt they'll give it much thought. In fact, they might thank us for it. If Becky finds herself some suitable mates, then that just means our clan will grow. We need some whelps in our folds if we are going to survive."

"You have a point."

We had reached the great bonfire. Ari was pushing her friend toward one of the other alphas. He was one of the strongest warriors and handled the front lines whenever there was a major battle. I could tell by his stance alone that he felt an instant connection. "Leave them be," I whispered in Ari's ear. "And let the chips fall where they may."

"Oh, come on, I have to see this." Ari protested.

"It's rude to stare." Vern backed me up and together we dragged her toward the elder hut.

As always, they were in the middle of a prayer. Patiently, we waited for them to finish. Only then did they look up and acknowledged us. "You have returned."

"We have," I answered. "And we have brought a new member to our clan." I motioned to the mark on her chest. "Last night, the Aetos attempted to imprint on her but we broke the bond."

Our leader rose to his feet. The headdress he wore seemed a little too big but he held it with poise as he shuffled over to us, relying heavily on the support of his staff. "Ah. Then it was a mark of true love."

I nodded. "We realized the risk."

"Were you aware you could have died?" He asked Ari.

"Yes. They told me."

"And you decided to mate with them regardless?"

"Yes."

The elder offered a smile. "Then you are indeed their one true mate." He lowered his head. "And I welcome you into our clan. We will begin the ceremony shortly. The clan sisters will assure that you are properly prepared."

"Thank you." Ari showed our leader her utmost respect, almost like she had been raised under dragon law all her life. "But may I have a moment with my mates?"

"Certainly."

We stepped outside.

"Is something wrong?" Vern was the first to ask.

"It's just... I've been thinking." She fidgeted with her fingers. "This ceremony is the okay for us to start having children, right?'

"Correct," I answered.

"And I want to have children, I really do, but... I'd like to wait a little bit."

"May I ask why?" I pressed, trying to get inside her head.

She ran her tongue across her lips, wetting them. "Well, I feel like there is so much I want to do with the two of you. I want to explore the world. I want to live my fullest life and a child, at least right now, would only get in the way of that." She shifted her weight to her opposite foot. "What I'm trying to say is that I'm not ready to settle down."

Vern stepped forward. "And that's nothing to apologize for. We'll wait as long as we need to until you're ready."

"We'll never force you to do anything," I added. "That is the difference between this clan and the Aetos. We listen to our women and do what is necessary to keep them happy."

"So, you aren't angry with me because I want to hold off on having kids?"

"Not at all," I assured her. "We will start our family when you're ready."

"Lucky, dragons have built-in birth control. If at least one of us pulls out, you'll never get pregnant." Vern chuckled. "And next time, it's your turn." He pointed at me.

"Hey, I'm the alpha here."

"Last time I checked, we were partners." Vern countered. "Which means it would only be fair if we switched off."

"He has a point," Ari said. "There's no need to be so greedy."

"It's not my fault," I whispered against her neck. "I just can't get enough of you."

Chapter 25 Ari

The clan sisters made me feel like royalty. A few of them brushed through my hair while a couple of artists painted my arms with a bright red dye. It reminded me of a henna tattoo I had gotten at a festival once, only this was much more ornate.

I watched them work, mesmerized by their skill. "Where did you learn to do that?" I asked.

"My mother taught me," the woman on the right answered.

"And she taught me." Other pointed at the first. "You see, I'm an outsider, just as you are but the clan is very loving and accepting. I felt like a member of the family in a short amount of time." She smiled. "Everyone helps everyone out. It's nothing like the outside work where everyone's at each other's throats."

I listened to her words. It was almost like she radiated with happiness. Was this what happened when a girl joined up with the dragons?

"There." They said in unison.

I examined their handiwork. "That's amazing."

"Now for your dress." They helped me slip it on. The fabric hugged my body in the most intimate of ways. It flowed beautifully, like living water lapping against my skin. "You look stunning," said the oldest woman. "You will make a fine addition to our clan."

I beamed at her compliment.

The final touch was for them to weave roses into my hair to symbolize the fiery blood now coursing through my veins. With that complete, I was led outside.

On my way to the great bonfire, I passed Becky. She waved and pointed excitedly at her newest catch.

I chuckled underneath my breath hoping she could find the happiness I felt.

There wasn't enough time to check out her partners because I was swallowed by the growing crowd. They urged me forward.

I held my breath as I saw the flames licking the sky and the eldest of the clan standing before them. He held a great big tome in his hands that looked like it must weigh a ton. Yet, despite his age, he held it with a steady hand.

He looked up. His eyes were a milky blue. If I had to guess, he was partially blind. "Come forth, my child." He beckoned with a wave of his wrist. He seemed to stare right into my soul, making me feel vulnerable.

My steps were small and shaky but I managed to reach my destination. It was then that I noticed that both Lyle and Vern were standing on the other side. They wore nothing but small pieces of fabric around their hips. Everything else was exposed from their broad hips to their muscular thighs. My face flushed as erotic thoughts flashed through my mind.

Not now, I chastised myself. Not in front of all these people.

But I just couldn't keep my eyes off them. They looked like Gods ready for battle. Their skin was bronzed and painted with the same design I had creeping up my arms.

The elder cleared his throat which helped direct my attention away from my attractive partners.

He opened his mouth and was about to say something but all of a sudden, a horrible gust of wind tore through the land, extinguishing the great fire.

Some of the women shrieked and pointed at the sky. "Aetos!" Someone called out.

Chaos exploded through the crowd as everyone scattered in different directions.

My eyes widened with horror as I watched one man getting swept off his feet and thrown into the air. A second later, a dragon rushed in and gobbled him up. I swear, I heard his bones crack.

Lyle picked me up and ran off with me. "What's happening?"

"We're being attacked," he said. "Aetos had this all planned, I am sure of it. Everyone has been gathered for the ceremony so our defenses were done."

"You mean, I caused this?"

"No," Vern added. "This isn't your fault."

"But if I hadn't..."

"Shh." He silenced me. "We're going to handle this. Don't you worry."

I glanced beyond Lyle's shoulder and saw the clan getting ripped apart. Horrible gusts of wind tore through houses while green-colored dragons terrorized all those who were defenseless.

"Now, I need you to stay here. Do not make a sound and do not come out under any circumstances. Do you hear me." Lyle looked me in the eyes. "I need you to help win this fight and I cannot do that if I am worried about your well-being."

"I can't just let you go out there and get yourselves killed!" I protested. "What if I never see you again?"

"Jeez, I thought you'd have a little bit more faith in us than that," Vern said, feigning offense. "We are trained dragons. We know how to hold our own in a fight."

Tears welled up in my eyes. "I'm just scared of losing you," I whispered. "I feel like I only just got to know you and now you're being ripped away from me."

He wrapped his arms around my body and held me close. "Nothing is going to happen to us. You just have to trust us on this one." He planted a gentle kiss on my lips. "Now, don't worry yourself too much. I don't want that hair of yours to go gray."

I punched his arm and he laughed.

"We will see you in a bit." Lyle kissed the top of my head. He then transformed into a dragon and off he went. I sunk against the cave wall and listened to the sounds of battle. I felt so useless and helpless.

There had to be something I could do to help.

But I was just a normal human girl. I couldn't sprout wings or spit out a fire.

I was completely and utterly helpless.

Chapter 26 Vern

Anger raged inside my soul. The Aetos were really getting on my nerves. First, they had tried to take away my mate and now they were threatening the safety of my people.

Despite my role as a beta, I did my part to protect the women and children. All those who opposed me were met with my marksmanship. That's right, dragons have guns too. They are pretty damn effective at piercing through dragon hide. All you have to do is aim at the right place and...

Bang!

I fired at an incoming Aetos, hitting their underbelly. The pain of it sent them crashing to the ground. Lyle was quick to swoop in and take them by the talons. The enemy dragon didn't stand a chance.

"Shouldn't you leave the fighting to the alphas?" Came a voice as vile as sewer water. I turned around and came face to face with Hector.

"You're the one behind this, aren't you?" Without another word, I held up my gun and fired. He was quick – quicker than I expected.

Before I could stop him, he had his hand around my throat. His fingers tightened in a choke hold as he lifted me off the ground. Desperate to free myself, I flailed my legs but they didn't make contact with his body.

I became lightheaded with the lack of air. My vision blurred.

Was this the end?

Hector laughed and it raised the hairs on the back of my neck. "I always knew you were pathetic, I just had no idea you were this bad. You're nothing more than a bug. And do you know what happens to bugs? They get squished."

At that moment, I managed to throw a good enough punch that it threw him off balance. He stumbled back and wiped the blood from his mouth.

On the ground, I gasped for air, unable to get up.

The tip of his boot came flying into my midsection. "I'm going to have so much fun torturing that mate of yours," he snarled as he kicked me again and again and again.

I coughed up blood. This guy was going to kill me and it seemed there was nothing I could do to stop him. That's when I spotted my gun. It was just within reach. I stretched out my arm only to have him stomp on my hand.

Pain shot through my joints. He had broken something, that much I was sure of.

"She was supposed to be mine, you know, but she wasn't really my type. I just wanted a reason to invade your clan. And it worked. Every alpha of the Aetos is at my disposal. They have killed countless of your members already."

"No..."

"Oh, yes." He leaned down and grabbed me by the chin. "And do you know who was one of the first to go? She begged for her life and pleaded with me but I couldn't stand that annoying little voice of hers, so I ended her right then and there." His smile became sinister. "I think her name was Jordan."

My eyes widened. "You bastard!" Hearing about the death of my sister made me lose it. A newfound strength coursed through me as I lunged at the enemy leader. I have no idea who took over at that moment but I hacked and I slashed until there was nothing left. Hector died choking on his own goddamn blood.

Lyle was forced to pull me away. "Vern." He said, his voice stern.

I was covered in blood and I could barely see. I had never felt so much hatred in my entire life. It threatened to consume me. Once again, I lunged toward the corpse, wanting to destroy every last inch of him.

An eerie sort of silence settled all around me. Even though I was cutting through bone and flesh, I could not hear myself. Lyle kept saying something but I couldn't hear him either.

A slow burning rolled through my body. I eased into it and embraced it as vengeance. Little did I know that my body was transforming. I became bigger and bigger. Scales lined my skin in a tightly woven pattern. My fingers transformed to talons the size of butcher knives.

I roared at the sky, causing the earth to rumble under my feet.

It was at that moment that I realized what had happened. I paused and looked down at myself, blinking in disbelief. I had gone through a full transformation.

"This is no time to gawk at yourself." I heard Lyle's voice inside my head.

"But... I'm a beta. I shouldn't be able to do this."

"In times of great stress, capable betas have ascended into the role of alphas." He recited as if reading from one of the elder scrolls.

"Wait... so that means."

"Yes. Ari is most likely in danger. We must go and save her." We tore through our enemies. Power surged through every inch of my new body. The Aetos started to flee. They had discovered the fate of their leader and they certainly did not want to fall in a similar manner.

At least some of them had sense.

Others did not.

They charged towards us, trying to slow our progress. All it took was a good swipe from Lyle to send them packing. And I was right there to finish them off.

"Where is she?" I searched the cave but there was no one there. The air was so thick with blood that there was no way for me to pick up her scent. "We told her to stay put."

"We must find her."

Chapter 27 Ari

There was a scream. It sounded oddly familiar.

Becky!

Without thinking, I ran out of hiding and headed straight toward the sound of distress. I couldn't just sit around while my best friend was slaughtered to death. It was my fault she had been brought to the clan, so she was my responsibility.

My lungs burned as I pushed myself to run as fast as I could. It was difficult to keep from stumbling when I didn't have any shoes on but, I continued forward.

Thorns and branches tore at my lovely dress.

"Help!"

I ran into a clearing and saw Becky trying to fend off a dragon. He held her with his wings, dangling her a few feet off the ground.

With little time to think, I picked up a rock and threw it as hard as I could.

He caught it in his hand and laughed. "Just the girl I wanted to see." He smiled, showing off a row of jagged teeth. "You know, you're the cause of all this death and destruction. We came all this way just to get you back."

"I'm not going anywhere." I planted my feet against the ground. "Now, I suggest you let go of my friend before you regret it."

The man crackled at my threat. "Is that supposed to scare me, little girl?" He threw Becky aside and her body crashed into a nearby tree. The blow was so catastrophic that a few of the leaves came spiraling to the ground.

I sprinted to her side. "Becky!"

"How touching." He mused. "You humans can be so sentimental. It makes me sick."

An ear-piercing shriek thundered through the woods as a blur of black shot forward. It took the man by surprise. Long, powerful claws dug into his sides. A dragon flew to the treetops and dropped its prey.

The man sped toward the ground but before he could fall to his death, he transformed into the biggest dragon I had ever seen. His scales were a vibrant shade of green. They shimmered in the sunlight as he stretched his wings.

"Run!" Came a voice in my head.

It was the smaller dragon.

"I'll fend him off. Find your mates. They'll protect you." The female voice urged. She craned her neck to look at me and that's when the green dragon made its fatal blow. All it took was a swipe of his talons to slice through her neck. There was blood everywhere. Some even splattered onto my dress.

My heart turned to ice when I realized I caused the death of one of my clan members. Anger clouded my judgment. I wasn't thinking clearly when I marched up to the hulking monster. "You're a scum. Do you hear me? Scum." I spat those words as if I could use them as weapons.

The dragon grinned, lips curling back to reveal his dagger-like teeth.

"Ari!" Becky hissed from behind. Apparently, she had regained her consciousness. "What the hell are you doing? Get back here."

"No." My voice trembled.

"Do you really think you can challenge me? I could crush you with a flick of my tail. You should be running for the hills."

"I am not a coward."

"Maybe so but you are certainly idiotic."

"Ari! I really think you should get away from that thing."

"Maybe you should listen to your little friend." Before I could do anything to stop him, he snatched up Becky and held her high above the ground.

"Let her go!"

"As you wish."

Becky screamed as she plummeted towards the ground. My eyes widened with horror as I realized that she would fall to her death. As unlikely as it was to succeed, I tried to align myself to catch her and break the fall.

She squeezed her eyes shut, preparing for her demise but it never came.

Instead, the dragon caught her and held her out of my reach again.

"What do you want?" I said through gritted teeth.

"And here I was thinking you'd never ask."

"I'm not here to play games."

"Neither am I." Answered the dragon. "Neither am I."

"Please..." Becky begged. "Don't drop me again. I'm way too young to die and I have a cat that I really need to feed. In fact..."

"Tell her to shut up."

"Becky, be quiet."

"Oh, um, okay. But if you could get me down from here that would be... well... appreciated." She looked down and gulped. "And if I could have that expedited –"

"I'm working on it." I interrupted before I turned my gaze to the dragon. "Now tell me what you want."

"My name is Nester. For years, I've been living the life of a beta due to the mistakes of my forefathers. You see, a long time ago, dragons were the rulers of breathtaking castles. These castles were filled with treasures. Humans were envious of these treasures and they would often lay siege in hopes of gaining the riches for themselves –"

"I'm not here for a history lesson."

He raised an eyebrow and brought Becky closer to his mouth. She screamed as his serpentine tongue lashed out, covering her in dragon saliva. "You will listen to what I have to say or risk losing this precious little friend of yours."

Bile gathered at the back of my throat.

Again, the feeling of helplessness began to consume me. Becky needed me and yet there was absolutely nothing I could do. I couldn't transform into a dragon. I couldn't fire a gun. All I could do was pray for a miracle.

"Now, as I was saying… Humans liked to try and steal from us but they were hardly a threat. They were easy to deal with. It was the other dragons that you had to deal with. And so, a member of Lyle's bloodline stole everything from my ancestor. Our family was left with nothing. We were left to roam the Earth with no place to call home. That is until the Aetos adopted us and gave us a place to stay. I have given up my life for vengeance."

"But Lyle was not the one who stole from you. Why should he pay the consequences?"

"Why then should I pay the consequences for mine." He hissed. "I have little authority despite the alpha blood that runs through my blood. I had to take orders from that likes of Hector – a weakling I was dying to crush underneath my heel. And yet, I bid time, waiting and waiting to make the perfect move."

I slipped my hand in my pocket and felt the smoothness of my phone. Perhaps, if I could contact Lyle and Vern somehow, they could come and put an end to this.

No.

I couldn't put them in danger. I glanced over at the fallen clan's member and my heart ached to know that she would never be returning to her family. What was she leaving behind? Mates? Children? Parents? Tears burned at the corners of my eyes. If only I had done something to protect her.

"So, I waited and waited until Lyle was the last living descendant. After he goes that dastardly family will be wiped from this planet and my forefathers will rest in peace. And I thought, why rush it? I had already waited so long, I might as well make him suffer."

This guy was the epitome of evil. He wanted nothing more than to hurt my mate – to torture him for crimes he hadn't committed. I couldn't stand it. My whole body shook.

"At first I thought that I would take you away and drive him to the brink of insanity but then I thought I'd kill two birds with one stone. I'd get you all to myself and start a war, warranting the Aetos the land they so rightfully deserve."

"You're never going to get away with this," I snapped. "My clan is much stronger than yours."

"Your clan?" He mocked. "You haven't even been accepted into the fold. What allegiance do you have with them?"

"They are the family of my mates and therefore –"

"Oh, spare me the grief." His voice echoed through my head. It was starting to give me a migraine. All I wanted to do was silence him for good. "Now, you have one of two options. Either you can come with me willingly and no one else has to get hurt or you can give me a hard time and this friend of yours and countless others will pay the price for it."

I locked eyes with Becky. She was crying. I could see the tears streaming down her cheeks. Maybe I was weak compared to the dragons all around me, but this was something I could do to save my friend – to save the clan. I had no idea what this madman was up to and honestly, I didn't want to find out. At least if I went along, I could find out what really made him tick and figure out his weakness. It was my only chance and I wasn't going to let it get away from me.

"Okay," I said.

The dragon smiled. "Perhaps you are smarter than you think."

He placed Becky on a high hanging tree branch. "Hey, what's going on?"

"Just stay calm, Becky, everything is going to be okay. Just stay where you are."

Nester transformed into a man and grabbed me by the hair. I waited until I was close enough and aimed my foot right at his crotch. He seemed to anticipate my move because he grabbed me by the ankle and knocked me off balance. I landed on my back, head slamming against the ground. I saw stars.

I tried to blink them away.

"You shouldn't have done that." He growled. "But if you rather do things the hard way then we'll do things the hard way." He pounced and the feeling of his body on top of mine made my stomach churn.

I fought him with everything I had but it wasn't enough. He overpowered me as Becky screamed at the top of her lungs, trying to notify someone – anyone – that I was in trouble.

"I think we're going to have a lot of fun together." I don't know where the rope came from but he wrapped it around my wrists so hard that it nearly broke through my skin. I flinched and all he did was laugh. This guy certainly knew how to play the role of a villain.

"Don't you dare hurt her!" Becky shouted as she hugged the trunk of the tree for dear life. If anyone was afraid of heights, it was her."

"She doesn't know how to shut up, does she?" He looked up. "I think maybe I should get rid of her after all."

"No!"

"Oh?" He raised his eyebrow. "You must care a lot about her."

"Do anything you want with me, just leave her alone. You do not need to drag her into this mess."

"Anything? Lucky me. I was going to have that anyway." He snickered as he picked me up and hoisted me over his shoulder like a sack of potatoes.

"You're not going to get away with this!" Becky tried throwing twigs at my kidnapper but it didn't do much.

I was taken away deep inside the woods where the trees loomed like giants and predatory eyes lurked from the shadows.

Please, I thought to myself. If anything, let this spare Lyle and Vern.

Chapter 28 Lyle

I stopped dead in my tracks.

Vern crashed into my backside. "What is it?" He asked, his voice full of worry as it filtered through my head.

"Ari is in serious danger."

It was then that Vern cocked his head to the side. His ears twitched slightly.

Then, I heard it too; someone's scream carried by the wind.

We exchanged a quick look at one another before running off toward the sound.

"Someone! Help! I need to get down from here!" The plea was repeated over and over again until I recognized who it was.

Becky.

We quickened our pace. Perhaps the two girls had found each other in the midst of the chaos.

"Damnit." Becky cursed as soon as she saw us. "Look, I'm just a regular ol' human. There's no need for you to kill me."

Vern shifted and held up his hands in a gesture of innocence. "Calm down, Becky, it's me, Vern. Where's Ari?"

As I listened, I walked over to one of my fallen clan sisters. So much blood had been shed on this day and it had all been my fault. I dragged my clan into this mess by being with Ari. Had I only kept my distance then maybe this could have been prevented.

"She was taken away by some creep. I don't know what they were talking about because the conversation was pretty one side, almost like she could hear him inside her head but I couldn't."

"That's because she could," Vern explained as he summoned his wings and flew up to rescue Becky from the tree. "Now, what did this guy look like?"

"He was this enormous green dragon." She pointed at me. "Bigger than you even."

"Did he ever transform into a man?" Vern asked.

She nodded. "Yes, towards the end when he took her away. He had copper colored hair and these really cold looking eyes. And I think he had a scar on his left cheek. It looked like a bite mark."

"A bite mark?" I thought.

"Hector's beta? But that wouldn't make any sense." Vern responded.

"Huh?" Becky looked between us, a look of confusion on her face. "What are you guys talking about."

Suddenly, my eyes widened. I shifted to my human form. "Hector was just a decoy."

Now it was Vern's turn to say, "huh?"

"Hector was the decoy. He never posed much of a threat. I mean, just think about it, you tore right through him. He didn't even try to put up a fight." I shook my head. "I should have seen this coming..."

"Lyle, you're speaking nonsense."

"Nester."

"How do you know his name?"

"Because our families have been at war for centuries. One of my ancestors took their land and they have been living as disgraced dragons ever since but if there's something we both know..."

"It's that dragons know how to hold a grudge." Vern finished for me. "So, you think this is all a plot for vengeance."

"That's exactly what is it," I said. "He's trying to get back at me by targeting the things I love. First my mate and now my clan."

"What direction did they go in?" Vern looked at Becky.

"Um..." She hesitated.

"Please," I begged her. "We have to find Ari. There is no telling what he might do to her."

"I think he went that way." She pointed due west. "No!" She quickly changed her mind. "That way."

I sighed. "Are you sure? This is very important. Ari's life might depend on it."

She gnawed on her bottom lip. "Yes, I'm pretty sure they went that way."

"Vern, take her back to the clan and make sure she is safe."

"I cannot leave you to handle this on your own. Ari is as much my mate as she is yours."

"I'm not here to discuss this with you," I said through gritted teeth. "This is my battle to fight and I will do it alone. I refuse to let you get involved."

"You stubborn bastard. Don't you get it? We're mating partners. Where you go, I go."

Becky raised her hand. "I can get back to the clan on my own. I think I know the way."

"It's too dangerous," I responded. "We have taken care of the majority of the Aetos threat but a few of them still lurk around the perimeter, trying to pick off our numbers. Ari would have my head if she knew I put you through any unnecessary danger."

"I can take care of myself," Becky protested.

"Not against dragons." Vern countered. "You're nothing more than an afternoon snack."

"I'm going. Catch up with me when you can."

"I don't like this," he said. "We should really go at this together. It would be safer that way."

I didn't bother to argue any longer. I eased into my dragon form and off I went. I hovered just above the tree line and used my superior vision to try and track any sign of footprints. If Nester had schemed this entire thing then he wasn't a fool. He'd have the wherewithal to cover his progress.

And yet, I was banking on the possibility that maybe he had made some sort of mistake.

Once I reached the waterfall, I swooped down and landed by the water's edge. My nostrils flared as I scanned the air for any trace of her scent. She had to be somewhere.

I was growing anxious. With every minute that passed, I was getting closer and closer to losing her and that was something I didn't want to think about. Just considering it brought a deep, penetrating ache to my heart. I steeled myself against it. Now was no time for emotions.

Where are you? I thought to myself. Where has he taken you?

"Ari…" It was a longshot but I tried to connect with her mind.

"Lyle?" Came her surprised response. "Is that really you or is this another one of Nester's tricks?"

A sigh of relief washed over me. If she was able to respond then it meant that she was alive. "Where are you?" I asked. "I'm coming to get you!"

"No." She answered.

"Don't be ridiculous, Ari."

"I'm not risking your life. This guy is absolutely insane. He wants to kill you."

"And he's going to kill you anyway if you don't tell me where he hid you."

"I refuse to let you die for my sake."

"I'm not going to die." I was starting to lose my patience with her. Didn't she understand the severity of this moment? "It's my job to protect you so please, just let me do that for you. I will never forgive myself if something were to happen to you."

Silence.

I paced along the edge of the lake. This was killing me inside. I should have been doing something to help her and yet, here I was – a sitting duck.

"Ari. Please."

"He brought me to this abandoned castle-looking place."

In an instant, I took to the sky. I knew exactly what she was talking about. "Stay put. I'm going to come and get you."

"Please, be careful." Even through our telepathic link, I heard the latent worry laced within her voice.

"I will. We're going to survive this, Ari. I promise."

My wings flapped with a vengeance as I forced myself to fly faster than I ever had before.

A thick fog had rolled over the landscape making it hard to see. There were a few times where I narrowly avoided crashing into a tree trunk.

I stayed focused and relied on my reflexes to get me safely to my destination.

Finally, I saw the castle emerge through the fog. It was crumbling, piece by piece. The moat had long since dried up and many of the watchtowers had fallen with time.

I landed before the open doorway. Nester was smart. To fight inside a castle meant that I could not rely on my dragon form. My size would only hinder me. So, if I wanted to get Ari back, I needed to do so on my own two feet.

Carefully, I crept forward. I kept to the shadows, hoping to use it as camouflage.

"You're wasting your time." Came a deep, menacing voice.

I stood up and rolled my shoulders. "Where is she?" I demanded as my eyes adjusted to the dim torchlight.

"She's in the other room, safe and sound."

I glanced at a wooden door.

Nester was quick to jump on my distraction. He dashed across the room, his body a blur. Before I could stop him, he had me pinned to the wall. "But let's not worry about her right now. There's some unsettled business we need to attend to." He dropped me to the ground and turned on his heels. As he walked from side to side, he played with a dagger. Its blade glistened with a deadly sharpness. "And we wouldn't want anyone to get hurt, now would we?"

"What do you want from me?" I stood my ground and examined my situation. If I wanted to win this fight, then I would need to be strategic about my every move.

"What do I want?" He chortled. "What I want is the return of my authority. I have lived as a beta for the better part of my life. No one respects me because one of my forefathers was too weak to defend what was rightfully his." He spat into the ground. "Now do you think that's fair?"

I took a step forward. "Let me propose something to you, then. We will have a fair fight, just the two of us. If you win, you can do as you wish. If I win, however, the Aetos will merge with the Ragnis and this war between the two will never rage again."

"You won't win," Nester said. "But I'll entertain your little wager." He held out his hand.

I didn't feel right in taking it but my honor forced me to do so.

He yanked me forward and drove his knee into my ribcage. I was left winded and disoriented. I lost my footing against the slick cobblestones, giving him yet another opportunity for attack. This time, he took me by the collar and threw me into a nearby column.

"I thought you'd put up a much better fight. This is turning out to be quite boring." He feigned a yawn as he advanced towards me.

That's right – walk right into my trap.

I coughed, trying to play up my injured status.

He squatted down beside me and grabbed me by the hair so I was forced to look at him. "And you call yourself an alpha? This is pathetic. That little mate of yours would be much better in my capable hands."

I lost it.

Nester looked surprised when I lunged forward and overtook him with the weight of my body. While on top of him, I laid down punch after punch after punch until there was a pool of his blood on the ground. Rage consumed me and I was hellbent on destroying this man. So long as I had a choice in the matter, he wouldn't live to take another breath.

Somehow, that dagger of his came into play. It sunk into my shoulder. My right arm hung limply with pain.

He pulled it out and jumped to his feet. We danced around one another.

"You're not going to win this," he said even with a mouthful of blood. "I will not let my family fall a second time."

"Perhaps there is a reason why they fell in the first place."

His eyes flashed with rage. The tip of his dagger grazed my cheek, leaving behind a thin cut. Blood stained my skin but I simply wiped it away. "See the problem is that you're working on vengeance and I'm working on love."

"Don't make me sick. You don't love that girl."

"And that's where you're wrong." I grabbed for his arm and pinned it behind his back, threatening to break it. The dagger fell from his hand as a crack echoed through the castle. "Now we're even."

He kicked away and panted. "This isn't over yet."

"Not by a longshot." I agreed. "But in the end, you'll be the one begging for mercy."

Chapter 29 Ari

I could hear everything that was going. I flinched every time I felt the castle shake. There had to be something I could do to put a stop to this madness.

Crash!

I held my breath and listened.

Was it over?

"Lyle?" I called out in my mind. "Please, answer me."

"I'm here." He assured. "You aren't going to get rid of me that quickly."

"What's happening out there?"

Dust dropped from the ceiling as the two men went at it. My heart tightened at the possibility that maybe Lyle wouldn't win this fight. He was doing everything he could to protect me and now I had to do the same for him.

"Vern?" I tried but there was no response.

I guess this was something I had to do on my own. I took a deep breath and focused on loosening the rope from around my wrists. If I could only free myself then I'd be able to do something – anything – to help Lyle.

The rope was tight – too tight. The more I wiggled my wrists together, the more it chaffed my skin. The smell of copper wafted up to my nose. Something warm and wet dripped over my fingertips. Despite the fact that I was bleeding, I continued my efforts but I was getting nowhere.

I opened my eyes and looked around for something that could help me make my escape. That's when I saw a jagged brick jutting from the wall. Maybe I could use that to cut through my bindings.

Sweat dripped down my brow as I bounced the chair over to that specific wall. I was terrified that one of the legs would break and that

I'd topple over but luckily, they held out long enough for me to reach the brick.

I had to hold my arms at an awkward angle to glide the rope along the jugged edge. My muscles screamed for a moment of rest but I did not listen to them. I needed to get us out of this mess.

Snap!

My wrists came free.

"Thank goodness," I muttered underneath my breath.

A second later, I was untying my legs. It felt strange to stand again. I steadied myself against a wall as a sudden wave of dizziness washed over me. I had never been a fan of blood. The smell was getting to me.

But I had no choice but to power through it.

I glanced around the room and spotted what looked like a spear. When I picked it up, it was much heavier than I had anticipated. It was difficult for me to keep it level. It didn't help that my palms were sweaty and covered with blood.

Nervousness threatened to cripple me. I couldn't do this. I wasn't a warrior. I was a goddamn secretary, for crying out loud.

"It's over, Lyle." Nester's voice dripped with venom. "You've been a lot of trouble but it'll all be worth it when I see that dying look on your face." A pause. "How is it going to feel to know that your mate has to live out the rest of her life with me? But don't worry, I'll take good care of her."

Lyle said something but his voice was so weak that I could barely understand his words.

My time was running out.

With no other choice, I adjusted my grip and went running out.

Nester looked up. "What the...?" That was all he was able to say before I rammed the tip of the spear into his chest. I thought for sure that would be enough to stop him but he simply ripped the spear from his body and marched towards me. His footsteps were thunderous and his eyes as black as night. I backed away until I hit a wall. There was nowhere left for me to go. "You have a death wish, don't you?"

"Don't you touch her!" Lyle shouted as he threw a dagger and its blade sunk into Nester's upper arm.

He roared as he staggered.

I took the chance to run to Lyle's side. He pushed me behind his body. "When I tell you to, I want you to run."

"I'm not leaving you behind."

"How touching." Nester mocked. "But let's be real here, neither one of you are going to survive."

Suddenly, I heard something. I cocked my head to the side trying to figure out what it was.

"Vern." Lyle smirked, lips stretching from ear to ear.

The castle rumbled as something landed on top of it.

I clung to Lyle as the roof threatened to collapse. In fact, a few of the bricks came tumbling down. Lyle held me in a protective embrace as the debris fell like rain.

The dying sun filtered through and the head of a dragon appeared.

It nudged Nester against the wall before snatching him up between his teeth.

"I wouldn't do that if I were you." Lyle said. "You'll be sick for months."

"You're right." I heard Vern say.

"Wait..."

"We'll explain later."

"Any last words?" Lyle walked up to his enemy who could not escape the killer jaws that now held him.

He spat in Lyle's face and that was the last straw. A plume of fire escaped Vern's lips, burning the man to a crisp. His ashes blew away with the wind.

I couldn't believe it. I sunk to my knees, crying.

Lyle was by my side in a second. "What's wrong?"

"I'm just relieved. We made it."

"I told you we would." He kissed the top of her head. "And we always will."

***

We arrived at the clan to find the remaining members hard at work. Some tended to the injured while others tended to the living. Those that couldn't stomach such things, worked to put out fires.

"It's destroyed..." I said aloud.

"We have risen from worse than this." Vern carried Lyle on his back. "Our clan is resilient."

"Was there no way we could have prevented this?"

"I'm sure there was but we cannot change the past. What has happened has happened." Vern seemed wiser now like the battle had aged him somehow.

We reached our hut and the roof had been torn off. The inside was in a state of disarray.

"Clear off the bed, will you?" He instructed.

I did as I was told. "Do you think he'll be okay?" I asked as he lowered Lyle onto the mattress. It pained me to see him so badly injured.

"Yeah, he'll be okay. It takes a lot to take him down."

"There's something I do not understand."

"And that is?" Vern spoke as he took a wet wash cloth and wiped away from of the blood from Lyle's face. I took one of my own and lifted his shirt. The fabric had started to dry into the blood. Carefully, I cut it away and pulled it free from his wounds. "There's some antiseptic in that chest over there." He pointed. "It'll hurt him but it'll help prevent infection."

I nodded and grabbed the bottle. Vern had to hold him down as I poured the liquid and watched it fizzle. His face was screwed up with pain. "Shh..." I whispered as I brushed my fingertips gently across his injured cheek. "Everything is going to be okay."

"So, what was it that you didn't understand?"

"Why did he come after me all by himself? Why weren't you two together?"

"Because we found your friend Becky and I had to bring her back to safety." After everything that had happened, I had forgotten about my best friend. "So, she's okay then?"

"Apart from a few cuts and bruises, yes, I'd say so." He squeezed the blood from a rag and sighed. "I told him to wait for me but he wouldn't hear it."

"He is pretty stubborn, isn't he?"

"You can say that again."

We chuckled.

"I think he felt the burden of bringing this on and causing all this destruction. He wanted to handle it himself but he forgets that we're partners and that we're supposed to keep each other safe."

"Well, I'm sure he really learned his lesson today," I said. "You really saved the day, Vern."

He shook his head. "There was so much more I could have done."

I rested my hand on his back. "You did what you could and that's all that matters. I don't think a single soul in this clan would blame you for what you did or didn't do."

Instead of soothing him, my words seemed to upset him. With this glassy look to his eyes, he left the hut.

Chapter 30 Vern

I walked through the clan, carrying on my shoulders a weight that dragged me down. Each step was a struggle. I slowed my pace as I approached my childhood home.

It was one of the few buildings that had been spared. The red paint my father liked to use was chipping away in a few places. He was getting on in years and accomplishing such tasks was becoming harder and harder. As his son, I was charged with helping him, but I had never found the time. I was always busy doing this or that. Most of the time, I was just goofing around.

Guilt tightened around my heart like a vice. It threatened to break in two when I walked inside. The atmosphere was somber and thick with remorse. I could smell death in the air and it made me sick. I wanted to run away.

When I stepped forward, a floorboard creaked underneath my foot, breaking the silence.

My mother turned to look at me, her eyes red and puffy. "Oh Vern..." Was all she said before she engulfed me in a hug. She trembled with sobs.

I wanted to say something but I was at a loss for words.

"Son." My father still loomed like the giant he was but his back had an arch to it that I hadn't noticed during my last visit. "It's good to see you."

I shook my head. "I should have been here to protect her."

"Do not blame yourself for her passing." My father spoke with a leveled voice. "Because of your actions, many others live to see another day." He leaned on his cane and nodded his head like he was about to doze off. "You were one of the few betas who took up the call to protect this place and you were rewarded for it."

"Rewarded for it?" I scoffed. "By losing my sister."

"You are an alpha now. You have an obligation to this clan. You are now one of its guardians but even so, that does not mean it is your responsibility to protect every single soul."

"But she was my sister." I could not ignore her any longer. With legs that felt like jelly, I approached her bed. She looked so peaceful with her arms crossed over her chest. If I didn't know any better, I would have guessed that she was just sleeping. "There was still so much I wanted..." I sunk down to my knees. "She will never get to meet her nieces and nephews. She'll never..." I buried my head in my hands. "I should have spent more time with her. Instead, I was always so caught up with other things."

My mother left the room, wailing.

"Vern."

Through tear-filled eyes, I looked up at my father. "She would have smacked you upside the head if she saw you acting like such a baby."

I couldn't help but laugh. My father had a point. "How did she... die?"

"Valiantly. She protected a group of children from certain death. Her sacrifice allowed them all to survive."

I nodded. "Then she did not die in vain."

***

The following morning.

Ari was by my side and I was glad for it. The warmth of her hand against mine helped to calm my emotions.

We followed the funeral march to the river where the water flowed with clear direction. It sparkled in the early morning sunlight.

Lyle squeezed my shoulder. "This is not goodbye," He said. "She will always be inside your heart."

I nodded. I was still grieving the loss of my sister but with the support of my mates, I knew I would get over it.

The elders chanted a song of farewell as the bodies of the fallen were pushed into the river. The boats that carried them were set aflame in Ragnis tradition.

Everyone bowed their heads and whispered prayers underneath their breaths. I was no different.

Then a drum was used to get everyone's attention. The clan elder stood atop a tree stump and held his staff high above his head before bringing it down three consecutive times. Thud. Thud. Thud.

"Today is a sad day indeed. Our numbers have been culled by a battle that has been brewing on the horizon for years. There are some of you that might want to take blame for what happened but do not think this way for your brethren would not agree with you." He held out his arms, motioning toward the crowd. "The Ragnis are a proud and powerful people and we stand together in the face of adversity."

Everyone nodded in agreement.

"Whatever threat might come our way, we will handle it – together." He smiled. "And while our numbers have been culled, today we gain new brothers and sisters through the Aetos. Some of you might be apprehensive about accepting our enemies as friends but with time we will join together and breathe as one."

The elders started up a cheer and soon everyone followed suit.

I looked towards the distance and watched as my sister floated away. I would never see her again and I just had to make my peace with that.

Ari squeezed my hand.

I smiled down at her. "Do you mind if we go back to the mansion for the night? I don't think I can stand to be here much longer."

Lyle nodded. "It might do you some good."

"Let me just find Becky."

We searched around and found her flanked by Astor and his beta, Julian.

"Did you want to go home?" She asked her friend.

"Actually... I think I might stay here a while. I promised I would help with some reconstruction..."

"You know you're a terrible liar, right?"

She blushed. "Oh, leave me alone, will you?"

Astor chuckled and wrapped his arm around her shoulders. "If you don't mind, we have some reconstructing to do."

Chapter 31 Ari

"Seems she's getting on well in the community." I said. For a change, I was riding on Vern's back. He was a bit smaller than Lyle but much, much faster. He tore through the clouds at lightning speed.

"Seems so. She might become your clan sister sooner than you think." He answered.

"Speaking of which, what's going to happen with our ceremony?"

"The elders will have to organize another." Lyle eased in beside us, riding a gust of wind that rippled through his wings. "We will let this event pass over and once the tides have calmed, you will receive your blessing."

"Is it bad that it worries me?" I outlined one of Vern's scales as I tried to gather my thoughts. "I mean, after what happened, what if they reject me? That Nester guy used me to start a war."

"So, Nester is at fault – not you." Vern said. "There is nothing for you to worry about. Everyone is going to love you."

***

We reached the mansion in record speed. The men marched right up to the second floor, dragging me with them. "Where are we going?"

"To take a bath." Vern looked back and offered a playful sort of grin. "I don't know about you but I'm filthy."

"Is the tub going to be big enough for three of us?" My question was answered the second I stepped into the bathroom. The place was extravagant. It belonged in a five-star hotel. The floor was made of a single slab of pink marble. The countertops followed the same scheme. "Is that a fireplace?"

"Yup." Vern burped and a bit of fire came shooting out of his mouth, igniting the wood. It crackled, adding a nice atmospheric touch.

Meanwhile, Lyle was bent over the tub and adjusting the temperature of the water. I couldn't stop myself from walking up behind him and running my fingertips along his back. He shivered with delight. "Quite a view from back here."

He chuckled and turned around, pulling me tight in his embrace. Our lips collided together. I was relieved to feel him alive and well when I had been so sure I was going to lose him. Relief washed over my body, lifting away the tension that had built up underneath my skin. I could finally breath again.

A lovely smell wafted into the air. I pulled away from the kiss to find Vern adding a bubble mixture to the water. "Aren't we a little too old for a bubble bath?"

"You're never too old for a bubble bath." He countered. "Besides, I want to see that lovely rack of yours nice and slippery." With that, he grabbed me by the hips and pushed me against the wall. He had a bit more fire to his touch than last time. Even his eyes burned with lust. Instead of following Lyle's lead, he was making a path of his own.

As his lips devoured mine, his hand slipped into my pants. "Mmm." He mumbled. "Someone's nice and wet." His lips traveled to the side of my neck as his fingers retreated to the outside of my panties. He pushed against it, teasing my pussy with the silky material.

I lifted my hips towards him but he pulled away.

"Vern..."

"What's the matter, baby girl?"

A shiver of delight ran through my spine. I loved it when he called me that. It made me feel special and loved.

He nibbled my earlobe and tugged on me.

"Mmm." I threw my head back and looked up at the ceiling. To my dismay, he removed his hand, leaving me unsatisfied. But a second later, that same hand worked its way underneath my shirt.

"We better get rid of this pesky thing," he said and, in a flash, he had ripped off my shirt. Next came my bra. The girls popped forward, eager to play.

Vern took the closest nipple into his mouth and swirled his tongue all around it. Occasionally, he would pause and blow softly onto my skin. As a result, I was covered in goosebumps.

"Ahem." Lyle was buck naked beside us. "I think it's my turn." He snatched me up and walked right into the tub.

"My pants!" I protested as they were soaked through.

"Oh, don't worry about them." He said as he rolled them off my body and threw them aside. They landed with a wet plop on the floor. Then went my panties. Lyle growled as he pulled me onto his lap. "How about we go on a little ride?"

I was more than eager to give him what he wanted. With my hands on his shoulders, I slowly eased myself onto his length. Somehow, he seemed even bigger. His cock stretched my every inch. Instead of bringing me pain, it was exactly what I needed to quell the fiery lust that burned inside of me.

Slowly, I worked up a pace until the water sloshed all around us.

Vern slipped in behind me and took my breasts into his hands. He kneaded them between his fingers until he found my nipples. He pinched them with a twist of his wrist.

I gasped and Lyle took his chance to kiss me. His tongue forced its way into my mouth where it tangled with mine. I fed off his passion and returned it with a hunger of my own. I had my fingers tangled through his hair, trying to pull him even closer.

Lyle grabbed me by the ass and guided me through the motions. I felt myself rising towards the edge but just when I thought I was going to climax, he stopped.

"Why...?"

He just grinned at me like he was up to no good.

"We're here to take a bath, remember?" Vern spoke up. He had a shampoo bottle in his hand. He squirted some of it onto his palms before lathering it into my hair.

I moaned. It felt divine to be pampered by such handsome men. As I floated on the surface of the water, Lyle ran his hands along my legs. His fingertips danced over my skin, teasing me with an innocent touch. That is, until he reached my thighs. He dared to go higher and higher but he never quite reached my aching mound. I wanted him so bad and yet I had the feeling that they were going to make me work for it.

Vern rinsed off my hair.

Before either man could do something else, I grabbed a bar of soap and ran it along Lyle's muscular body. I made sure to give every inch equal attention.

"That feels good." He said as he ran his fingers through my thick hair. "But don't forget to give Vern some attention or he might get a little jealous."

"Oh, don't worry, I'll make sure to take good care of him." I turned around and pushed him into a seated position. I abandoned the soap and wrapped my fingers around his raging cock. I squeezed it until he groaned. Only then did I start my up and down motion.

"You're such a tease," he said through gritted teeth.

"I can say the same for the two of you," I whispered against his ear as I ran my thumb across his tip. He jerked with pleasure so I did it again and again and again until I was sure he would lose his mind.

But then the tables turned.

He picked me up and sat me down on the edge of the porcelain tub. The cool air above the water made my nipples perk up almost to a painful degree but Vern didn't care about them. He dove between my legs and drank his fill. His tongue was much quicker than Lyle's. It flicked back and forth against my clit.

I gripped the windowsill, trying to keep back the wave of pleasure. The longer I held back my orgasm, the better it would feel.

He flipped me around and ate me out from behind. His tongue traveled the entire length of my lips. He parted them and explored inside, tasting me straight from the source.

My legs had begun to shake, and my toes curled as I screamed with pleasure.

He stopped.

I groaned.

"What's the matter?" He was toying with me.

"Why did you stop?" I asked as I panted for breath.

"Because I think Lyle needs a bit of attention." He said with a toss of his head.

Lyle had his cock in his hand. He stroked it slowly. Even through the water, I could see how unbelievably hard it had become.

"Stand up," I said. It surprised me how demanding I sounded but at this point, my hunger was much too great.

I got down on my knees before bringing his tip to my mouth. My tits floated on the water as I leaned forward and eased his first few inches down my throat. It was difficult to do when he was so massive. It almost felt like my jaw would come unhinged.

But bent on pleasuring him, I started to bob my head. I was slow about it at first, wanting to torment him the way he had done to me.

My tongue swept along his underside, targeting his most sensitive of places. When that wasn't enough to drive him made, I started to fondle his balls.

"Mmm." Was all that he said as he took my face in both his hands. He pounded his cock into the back of my throat repeatedly.

Drool dropped down to my breasts as I tried to accommodate his size.

When it was too much, I pulled away, gasping for air.

"The water's getting cold. How about we step out?" Vern suggested as he pulled the plug.

I wanted to protest. That couldn't possibly be the end of our fun. None of us had climaxed. My pussy yearned for release and I had half a mind to reach between my legs and rub one out.

But then Vern wrapped a warm towel around my body. He dried me off while Lyle tussled my hair.

"How did I ever get this lucky?" I whispered aloud even though I intended to keep that thought to myself.

Lyle smiled. "I would argue that we are the lucky ones here. We found ourselves the most beautiful mate in all the world."

Vern nodded in agreement. "I'd say we hit the jackpot."

They kissed my cheeks. "Now, shall we retreat into the bedroom. We're all horribly tired." Lyle spoke with a strange sort of tone like he was trying to hide something.

"You mean you want to go to bed?" I asked. "But its not even noon."

"I don't know but I could use a nap right about now." Vern added. "I'm beat."

I looked at the two of them. They were definitely up to something.

Nonetheless, I allowed Lyle to carry me over to the bedroom. The silk sheets felt amazing against my skin. So, I cuddled against it and found a home for myself on Lyle's chest. He ran his hand along my spine, tickling me slightly.

I fidgeted.

"Gotcha." He said as he attacked my sides.

I laughed and curled up into the tiniest of balls. I tried to escape him but he just continued to tickle me.

Then, to make matters worse, Lyle joined in on the torture.

There was nowhere for me to go.

"Please…" I begged as I started running out of air. "Stop!"

"Hmm, I'll think about it." Vern chuckled as he scooped me up and deposited me onto his body. "And maybe if you do me a little favor."

"What's that?"

"A favorite number of mine." He said with a devilish grin. "Can you guess what it is?"

I furrowed my brows together. What was he talking about?"

"69."

Chapter 32 Lyle

Seeing Vern take control was way more lust inducing than I thought it was going to be. I was so accustomed to taking the reigns that I had never stopped to consider what it might be like if I took the backseat.

I watched as Ari spun around and took my mating partner's member into her mouth. Those perfect little lips of hers wrapped around him so tightly that it created a vacuum as she bobbed her head up and down. As she got into the movements, she wiggled her hips from side to side.

This woman was the pure definition of sexy, I thought.

Just the sight of her was enough to make me explode.

My hand found its way around my girth where it slid easily along my length. I added some lube to make it even easier. Plus, by doing so, my fingers would be nice and ready to explore her asshole. This thought forced my hand to move at a faster pace. If I wasn't careful, I was going to climax right then and there.

So, I stopped and interrupted their sex position.

"Hands and knees." I ordered and she was quick to obey. "Good girl." I purred as I ran my hand along her ass cheek. I passed it between her opening until my middle finger found her entrance. I probed it and she tensed slightly.

Vern shimmied his way underneath her and once against took her mound into his mouth. As his tongue shot in and out of her pussy, she became distracted. I waited for her back to arch before ramming a finger inside her tightness.

She jerked away but I held her firm by the shoulders. She had nowhere to go. She was now my little plaything.

My finger moved in and out of her at a slow, deliberate pace. I wanted to make her lose her mind.

"Do you like that?" I whiskered against her ear. "Having two men pleasure you at the same time?"

"Yes!" She screamed.

I smacked her ass and she screamed even louder. "I didn't hear you."

"Yes!"

Abruptly, I shoved another finger into her hole. She squeezed against them but I made room for them to explore her insides.

"Why don't you tell us what you want us to do to you?"

"Fuck me!"

"Such a naughty girl," I taunted. "Good girls don't ask men to fuck them."

"I'm a bad girl..." She huffed.

"But bad girls get punished." I told her as I bit her ass, leaving behind a mark. "Do you want to be punished?"

She did not answer me. Her eyes had rolled into the back of her head. She was on the very tip of an orgasm and that's exactly when both Vern and I stopped our ministrations. She collapsed onto the bed.

"I'll take it from here," Vern said, switching places with me.

He yanked her to the edge of the bed and bent her over the edge. With her ass at the perfect height, he lined up his cock. All he needed was one good thrust.

But instead, he teased her. He had her clit between his thumb and forefinger, rolling it back and forth, faster and faster.

Ari moaned to the high heavens.

I took my place in front of her. She immediately leaned her head down to greet my member with her adoring lips. She sucked on my tip, swirling her tongue all around. Then that lovely tongue of hers swirled a path down to my balls where she lingered for a while.

Suddenly, Vern plunged inside her depths. He grabbed a fistful of her hair and pulled her head back, making it impossible for her to continue her blowjob.

As Vern fucked her, that incredible rack of hers kept swinging back and forth. I just couldn't stop myself from making a move.

I worshiped her tits, kissing every single inch of her soft mounds. When I got around to her nipples, I toyed with them. Occasionally, I would bite down just to see the look on her face.

"Cum for us, Ari." I whispered in her ear. "Go ahead."

She screamed at the top of her lungs as her whole body began to shake. Vern groaned with the pleasure of it. He slumped forward, his balls now emptied.

I waited for him to step aside.

"I hope you're ready for round two."

She gasped as I slipped between her ass cheeks. My cock was already nice and lubed up making the process much easier.

Her toes curled as I kept going deeper and deeper.

"You're so big..."

I kissed her back and made her feel loved as I rocked against her body. I took my time, wanting us to both enjoy the experience of being together. "Does that feel good?" I asked as I went a little faster.

"So good." She was grinding her hips against the side of the bed. I loved the fact that she was so damn naughty. Oh, we were going to have a lot of fun together.

My balls started to slap against her pussy as I pushed myself a little harder. I still wasn't going fast but I was definitely going hard.

She moaned. "I'm going to cum."

"Then cum for me." I nibbled at the side of her neck. "Let me feel you shaking around my cock."

And that's exactly what happened. Her insides tightened, holding me in a vice grip. I tried to pull out as the feeling of orgasm crept along my length. I was on the very edge of exploding but she was so damn tight that I couldn't do anything about it. I lost all control, coating her insides with my sticky cum.

She gasped and buried her head against the sheets.

Vern and I exchanged a look of mutual understanding. Ari would soon be carrying our child. I just prayed she was ready for it.

I pulled out and saw that she was dripping. I carried her to the bathroom and helped get her clean. Vern was there to get her into some pajamas.

"That was amazing," she said with a smile.

Neither one of us said a word.

Once we were back in bed, I took her hand and looked into her eyes. "Do you understand what just happened?"

"We had the best damn sex of my entire life?"

"Well, yes... there's that." My mouth suddenly felt dry. I was terrified that she would respond with anger or that she would demand we get rid of the baby.

"Lyle?"

"I wasn't able to pull out." I said at last. I turned my head and looked away for a moment before returning my gaze to that beautiful face of hers. "Which means..."

"I'm pregnant."

I nodded.

She took a deep breath. "Okay."

"Okay?" I repeated.

She smiled "Okay."

Vern cocked his head. "Mind telling us what your thinking right now?" He sat down beside us. "We know you said you wanted to wait."

"It was an accident," she said. "Besides, I think I am ready now." She fidgeted with the sheets before straightening out her posture. "The battle between clans really taught me something. Life is much too short to wait."

She took both our hands and squeezed them.

"So, I don't want to wait any longer. I want to start a family with you two." Her smile deepened. "You have shown me a world I never imagined could exist and it's a world in which I'd be honored to raise a child."

Vern rested his ear on her stomach. "What do you think it'll be? A boy or a girl?"

"I'd like a girl," she answered. "Although she'll have a hell of a time dating when she's a teenager. If I had to guess, you two will be the sort of fathers to chance away every boy from our doorstep."

"That's right." Vern chuckled. "In fact, I should go out and buy my shotgun right now. I think it'll be a pretty sound investment, don't you think?"

I shook my head. "I'd like a boy."

"Alright but once puberty comes around that's on you two." Ari held up her hands. "I have no idea how to handle hormonal dragons."

I laughed. "Just as you would handle a hormonal human. You sit them down and explain to them that girls are to be respected and cherished."

Ari leaned forward and kissed my lips. "You two are going to be pretty amazing fathers."

"And you, an amazing mother." I responded as we fell into bed. She wrapped her arms around me while Vern spooned her from behind. She yawned and closed her eyes. "Sweet dreams," I whispered as I kissed the top of her head.

"I love you."

My heart skipped a beat. It was the first time she had said those three little words and it meant so much to hear them coming from her lips. I hugged her tight, vowing to protect her and our unborn child until my last dying breath. "I love you too."

Chapter 33 Ari

The following Sunday.

I was once again in a ceremony gown. This time it was a lilac color. It was styled like the tunic of a Greek Goddess and it certainly made me feel like one.

"You look beautiful." Becky clapped her hands together as she fussed with a particular flower and the way it laid against my hair. "Who would have thought we would end up here. It feels like just the other day when I was helping you pick out clothes for that big interview of yours and now, you're getting married."

"I'm not getting married," I corrected even as my cheeks turned red with the thought. "Dragons don't get married."

"Well, this is as close as you're going to get so enjoy it." Becky squeezed my arms, accidentally smudging some of the dye. "Oops."

"Do not worry." Said one of the artists. "They say whoever is blessed with the ceremonial dye will receive it next."

"Do you hear that?" I nudged her with my elbow. "You're up next."

She held up her hand as if to hide the mating mark on her chest but I knew it was there.

"Since when are you the shy one?" I asked, raising an eyebrow. "You should be happy you landed one of the strongest warriors in the entire clan. And I hear Julian is quite the marksmen."

"Oh, yes. He shot an apple off my head the other day. I thought for sure he was going to kill me but he was right on target." She giggled. "I definitely owe you one."

"I'll remember that when I need a babysitter."

Her eyes widened. "Don't tell me..."

I nodded.

She jumped for joy. "Oh! That's wonderful." Suddenly, she stopped. "Wait. How does that work exactly? Are they human babies or do you lay an egg? I mean, technically speaking, dragons are just giant lizards."

The other members of the clan gasped in horror. "We most certainly are not just giant lizards." Chastised the matriarch. "We are a noble species and you will treat us as such."

Becky gulped.

"Come, the time has arrived." The matriarch took my hand and guided me through a doorway of stringed beads. As soon as I stepped into the sunlight, I shielded my eyes against the brightness. Luckily, that meant I was also shielded from the confetti of broken up seashells in my direction. They rained down and caught the light, casting shadows every which way.

All around me, members of the Ragnis along with members of the Aetos smiled. They clapped as I walked by. A few even whispered their own blessing.

The matriarch weaved her way to the great fire and there I was reunited with my mates. Once again, they were wearing nothing but a strip of fabric around their waists. My cheeks burned as a few fantasies recycled through my thoughts.

"We are gathered here today to formally welcome two of our newest members."

Two? I wondered to myself. Was Becky having this ceremony alongside me but as I looked around, she was lingering on the sidelines with Astor and Julian.

"Ari Greene will from this moment forward be recognized as Ari Stokes as she joins in union with our alpha. Lyle has done everything to protect us and now he has a new task at his feet – to protect his family."

A piece of wood was burned and the smoke was the same color of purple as my dress.

It was passed to me and then along to my mates. Vern held it above his head before throwing it into the bonfire. The flames shifted from yellow to purple and the whole crowd fell into silence.

The elder tapped his staff and I looked up at his milky eyes. "She carries their child and may that child join this world in health and happiness." He paused and locked his gaze with mine. "And may Ari carry on many more children to come."

This time I was offered a chalice. I drank what was inside and it warmed my system. In a way, I felt like I could jump up and fly.

"May all four of you live blessed lives." With that, the combined clan members erupted into applause.

Vern swept me off my feet while Lyle rested his hand on my stomach.

***

The rest of the day was filled with dancing and celebration. I had never danced so much in my entire life. Even after my feet had gone numb, Lyle and Vern continued to twirl me around.

It was a mission to try and escape. But when I did, I found an incredible assortment of food lined up on a buffet table. I'm going to blame it on the pregnancy but I stuffed myself silly. Everything looked so good that I had to try it all from the roasted chicken to the blueberry pie.

"Enjoying yourself?" Vern asked as he sat down beside me.

I had found a little safe haven underneath the leaves of a willow tree.

"You know, I think I could get used to this."

He leaned back. "I could do without all the dancing."

"I thought you liked dancing."

"I do but I like doing you more."

I laughed. "Is that all you think about?"

"I'm sorry but I'm a man and 90% of my thoughts consist of undressing you and having my way."

"And the other 10%?"

"Food."

I laughed even harder. "This is why I love you."

Lyle appeared with a plate. It was piled high with all kinds of different desserts.

"Jeez, someone has a sweet tooth." I teased.

"Why do you think I enjoy eating you out so much."

"Lyle." I chided. He was practically shouting it to the world. "Do you want everyone to hear you?"

He shrugged. "What do I care? As far as I'm concerned, I have the most beautiful girl in the world and I deserve to brag about it."

I shook my head. "Sometimes, you two are too much."

"You wouldn't trade us for the world," Vern said.

"You got that right."

Epilogue Ari

A few years later.

"We should have left fifteen minutes ago." I shouted through the house as my little one, Tyson, held my hand. The tiny wings on his back fluttered as he attempted to fly. He made it off the ground a few inches before he landed with a thud.

I shot him a look and he just averted my gaze by playing with his stuffed monkey.

Finally, Vern came down the stairwell. He was looking as handsome as ever. He smiled and planted a kiss on my cheek. "Hey there, beautiful." Even after all our time together, his words sent butterflies fluttering through my stomach.

"Have I ever told you that you're cute when you blush?"

"Only a million times or so."

Tyson tugged on his father's pant leg. "Daddy!" He said as he made grabby hands toward the dragon.

Vern scoped up his son and tossed him into the air. Tyson giggled with glee.

"Careful!" I chided when Tyson came dangerously close to hitting the ceiling fan.

"Don't listen to her, little guy." He waved off my concerns. "Now, flap those wings just like daddy showed you."

Tyson screwed up his face and for a split second, he hovered in place. His little wings struggled to keep him afloat.

With a huff, he lost his focus and came crashing down.

I screamed.

Thankfully, Vern caught him, safe and sound. "Just between you and me, mommy is a worry wart." He whispered as he covered his mouth with his hand as if that would stop me from hearing him.

"I've told you a million times not to do that. You could end up hurting him one of these days."

"He's a dragon. He's a little more resilient than a normal baby."

"That doesn't mean you can go off and throw him to Timbuktu."

"Nice place."

"Huh?"

"What are you two bickering about?" Lyle's booming voice echoed through the foyer. The second Tyson heard it, he ran forward and jumped into his arms.

Lyle smiled and hugged him tightly.

"Hey there, little buddy. How're those wings?"

Tyson gave them a little shake.

"You'll be flying in no time."

"That's what I'm worried about." I mumbled underneath my breath. "He's enough of a handful when he started to walk. I can only imagine what's going to happen when he starts to fly. How am I supposed to get him down when I have another bun in the oven?"

"I already told you that I would stay home and help you raise the children." Vern came up behind me and wrapped his arms around my swollen belly. "So, quit your worrying or you're going to drive yourself to an early grave."

Lyle cleared his throat. "Shall we get going?"

I raised an eyebrow. "Why are you wearing a suit?"

"I have a meeting I need to go to after we're done with the clan. One of my investors is thinking about opening up another branch in Europe and we need to brainstorm the logistics."

"Always working," I said as I tidied up his lapel. "Can't you think about anything else?"

"I can name a few things." He said as he grabbed my ass and gave it a little squeeze.

I slapped him away. "Not in front of Tyson," I hissed.

Tyson cocked his head to the side.

"Let's just go. I'm eager to meet Becky's baby." I said as I opened up the door to the garage. Despite their ability to fly, it was easier to travel by car whenever Tyson was with it. He had a habit of squirming out of my grasp whenever we reached a certain altitude. Lyle assured me it was normal but you try dropping your baby from a thousand feet!

***

"Oh, she's precious." I picked up the newborn and cradled her in my arms. "Absolutely precious. And she has your eyes, Becky."

She smiled. "And Astor's wild hair."

I ran my fingers along the thick shock of black. "You're going to cause mommy and daddies a lot of trouble when you grow up."

Tyson rose on his tippy toes trying to see the baby. "What is it?" He asked.

"A baby," I explained. "She'll grow up to be a dragon just like you."

He knitted his brows together.

"He's getting big." Becky adjusted herself on the bed so she could sit up a little straighter. Julian was there to fluff up her pillows and make her as comfortable as possible.

"He is," I said as I ruffled his hair.

He pouted and ran off to hide behind his father. Lyle placed a hand on his head. His phone started to ring and I thought he would answer it but instead he ignored it. "It's not everyday that you get to see a newborn whelp. The occurrence has become rare and it's a shame."

"Do you think dragons will ever become... you know, extinct?" Becky blurted out.

I made the 'cut it out' gesture but she didn't see me.

"Perhaps one day." Lyle said, his tone serious. "After all, nothing can last together but I believe our legacy will live on to eternity. There will always be stories about dragons."

I passed the baby into her mother's arms. "And until that day, we all have to do our part to keep the race alive." I said with a wink. "So, no slacking!"

"Oh, I don't think that'll be a problem." Vern grinned.

Becky laughed. "They really are a horny lot."

"Tell me about it." I sat down on the edge of the bed. "Do you guys think we could have a minute?"

"Of course." Astor nodded his head and out they went.

Once we were alone, I turned to Becky. "How did we end up here?"

"I don't know but I don't regret it for a second. Joining this clan was the best thing that has ever happened to me." As she spoke, she looked down at her child.

"I know exactly how you feel," I whispered. "And I'm just glad that some fairy tales really do come true."

*****

*****

Don't miss out!

Visit the website below and you can sign up to receive emails whenever Lilly Wilder publishes a new book. There's no charge and no obligation.

https://books2read.com/r/B-A-KAQD-UPVIC

BOOKS 2 READ

Connecting independent readers to independent writers.

Also by Lilly Wilder

Indebted To The Vampires
Wolf's Nanny
Bearly Familiar
Protected by the Wolves
Academy For Vampires
Bear Protection
Dragon Dreams
Seduced by Dragons
Her Lion Protectors